By Sophie Snow

SOPHIE SNOW

First published in 2024 by Sophie Snow
This paperback edition first published in 2024

First Edition

Copyright © 2024 by Sophie Snow

The moral rights of the author have been asserted.

Proofreading by Nina Fiegl.
Character illustration by badeyart.

ISBN: 978-1-7394450-7-2 (paperback)
ISBN: 978-1-7394450-8-9 (eBook)

*For anyone who's ever picked up a romance book
and unlocked a new kink along the way.*

Happy Santa season!

Content Warnings

Naughty or Nice is an adult novel that features explicit content and some topics that may be triggering for some readers. The following is a list of topics featured in Naughty or Nice:

Alcohol, cheating (past relationship), climate change, divorce, explicit language, explicit sexual content (accidental unprotected sex, anal play, biting, breeding kink, cum play, dirty talk, face sitting, fingering, fingering while driving, grinding, mutual masturbation, oral sex, PIV penetration, public sexual activity, sex toys, and santa kink,) injury, job loss, pregnancy, sexism.

You can read about these content warnings in more detail at www. sophiesnowbooks.com.

1
RORA
December 3

"**I**s there a reason you want me dressed like I'm starring in low-budget Christmas porn?"

I stare in horror at the green velvet mini skirt, top, and candy cane striped stockings my best friend is clutching. Noelle hands them to me, frowning. "Low budget? I paid a hundred dollars for this."

When I hold the skirt up to my body, it's tiny. "You overpaid. Seriously, Noelle, this is obscene. It's so short my ass is going to be on full display." I can't tell without trying it on, but I'm pretty sure my cleavage will be too.

She tosses a matching scrap of velvet at me, which lands atop the camera bag slung over my shoulder. "There are shorts."

"This is underwear."

"Potayto, potahto."

I bunch the fabric up and look around The Enchanted Workshop warily. Noelle's family loves Christmas—like, *loves* Christmas. So much so that they moved to Wintermore over twenty years ago, specifically to open up a toy store. It's my first time back here for Christmas since I left for college, but I don't remember things being quite so … sexy.

"This is a toy store. The children don't need to see me half naked when I take their pictures with Santa."

"Maybe not, but you're hot, and I'm not above dressing you

in next to nothing to convince their parents to spend more money."

Ah, capitalism.

"Do you really think your dad will be cool with this?" I hold up the sad excuse for a dress.

Noelle's dad, Charlie, has been The Enchanted Workshop's Santa every year since they opened, and he's practically a second dad to me.

"About that." She grimaces. "My dad's not playing Santa this year. He was trying to hang more Christmas lights on the house and fell off the roof yesterday morning. Broke both his legs." She says it matter-of-factly, like falling off the roof is a regular occurrence.

"Oh my god, is he okay?"

Noelle waves a dismissive hand. "He's fine. The breaks were clean, and he was discharged this morning." I must look as worried as I feel because she rushes on. "He's in great spirits. He says he's in his *The Santa Clause* era and made me bring his laptop to the hospital last night so he could watch it in bed."

The tightness in my chest eases. If Charlie's still up for Christmas movies, he's probably okay. I make a mental note to stop by the Whitten house to visit Charlie and Noelle's mom, Kate, after the store closes.

Speaking of which…

Today is the first Saturday of December, which is the first day of the month kids can meet Santa and have their picture taken. It's the store's busiest time of the year, and people come from all over western Wyoming to meet Santa and buy toys. The Whittens have stuck to the same schedule since they opened, and I can't imagine them canceling so last minute.

"Who's going to be Santa? Felix?"

Noelle clenches her jaw. "As if we could count on my darling brother to actually show up and not disappoint the kids."

I wince. Felix is technically the store manager, but I know Noelle picks up most of the work he should be doing.

"My uncle, Henry, is flying in, thank god. He should be here any minute."

"Your uncle who lives in Greenland?" I ask, and Noelle nods. "He's flying, what, four-thousand miles? To play Santa?" Hard as I try, I can't entirely hide the disbelief from my voice.

"He was already coming for Christmas. He only had to pull his flight forward a few days, and he's bringing his own Santa suit."

His own Santa suit. Jesus. I've never met Charlie's brother, but I'm not surprised he has his own suit. The whole Whitten family is Christmas-crazy.

Every second standing in the toy store is a glaring reminder of why I avoid my hometown of Wintermore, Wyoming at this time of year: this whole town is Christmas-obsessed. It has been since a popular Christmas movie used it as a backdrop when I was seven, and upon the movie's release, tourists started flocking to Wintermore for the holidays.

The quiet, quaint town my parents fell in love with when they moved here to raise me is long gone. These days, Wintermore is nothing but a tourist trap disguised as a Winter Wonderland, and I make a point to visit only during the warmer months.

It's not the first time Noelle has asked me to come home for Christmas, but it's the first time she's begged. Their usual Santa photographer pulled out, and the timing was perfect, considering she called the day after I was fired from the photojournalism job I'd had for six years. But I would have come for her even if I hadn't been fired. She's family.

At least it's familiar; I shot The Enchanted Workshop's Santa pictures all through high school. Still, there's no nostalgia as I look around the toy store, just dread and resignation that, in a couple of hours, this place will be teeming with rowdy holiday shoppers making a mess of Noelle's carefully stacked shelves.

I can see how hard she's worked to get this place in shape for the start of the season, and it's that—and only that—that has me grabbing the *shorts* from where they've fallen on the floor. "I'll wear it this weekend, but I'm ordering something with more fabric."

"Deal," Noelle agrees with a shit-eating grin. "You can change in the back room." She darts away before I can change my mind, busying herself with a crooked bough of holly hanging in the window.

I sigh and push through the squeaky door behind the counter. Even the staff-only hallway is decked out with twinkling lights and huge red bows. A massive Christmas tree towers in the corner of the tiny back room, its branches weighed down with too many ornaments to count.

It would be easy to assume it takes them weeks to put their Christmas decor up every year, but they keep it up year-round. The Whittens moved from Central Texas to Wintermore because of our town's Christmas obsession, and they fit right in. They are, admittedly, the only thing I don't mind about it all.

I strip off my leggings and sweatshirt, and pull on the skirt and candy cane stockings. And the shorts, of course. I groan, inspecting myself in the mirror stuck on the back of the door. With my lacy red bra, I look like I've just stepped off the pages of the Christmas issue of *Playboy*: hot, but not exactly toy store friendly.

I reach for the tiny green shirt I dropped on my bag as the door clicks open. Good. Maybe Noelle will see sense when she sees this on a human body.

"I don't think I—" I stand up and stop in my tracks as I turn around.

Not Noelle. *Definitely not Noelle.*

My mouth goes dry as I take in the man standing in the doorway. He's wearing red velvet pants and nothing else. Aside from chestnut leather suspenders and tattoos scrawled across his pecs, his chest is bare. He has a red jacket, a white shirt, and a duffel bag slung over his arm, but I can see more ink peeking out. The man is fucking gorgeous, and my eyes haven't even made it past his torso yet.

When I finally drag my gaze to his face, my eyes widen. He has piercing blue eyes, and his cheeks are scarlet from the cold. His salt-and-pepper hair is windswept, but his short beard is flawless.

It isn't until I clock his expression, as stunned as I feel, that I remember I'm standing in front of him in nothing but a bra and a sorry excuse for a skirt. I hold the green velvet shirt over my chest, and he blinks, looking away as my movement breaks the tension between us.

He clears his throat. "I'm so sorry. I spilled coffee on my shirt, and Noelle said I could change back here. She didn't mention anyone would be here." He has a strong Texan twang that's all too familiar to my ears, but his voice is much deeper than his brother's.

I swallow. *How did I not know Noelle's uncle Henry looked like this?*

"Don't worry about it. I was just finishing up."

"Right. Shit." He turns around, the tips of his ears blazing red, and I take a deep breath once his back is to me.

I quickly pull the velvet shirt on. "I'm decent." I look down at myself and shake my head. I might as well be wearing nothing. "Decent might be pushing it, actually," I grumble. When I look up, he's facing me again. His gaze quickly jumps from my chest to my face. "Noelle picked it."

His throat bobs. "It's very … festive."

"That, it is. You must be Henry."

He nods, setting his bag on the floor and reaching to shake my hand. "The accent gave it away, huh?"

His hand is warm in mine. *Holy shit, it's massive.* I swear he could hold both of my hands in one of his with room to spare.

"The Santa suit helped. I'm Rora. Aurora Stanley. But Rora is fine," I ramble before pressing my lips together so I don't continue speaking.

Henry squeezes my hand once more and gently lets it go. "The famous Rora. I've heard a lot about you over the years." His smile is so blinding I have to look away, pretending to brush a spot of lint from my skirt.

"Likewise," I say, though at this point, all I can remember about him is that he's a climatologist, working in Greenland, or something like that. And he's Noelle's uncle, so it really shouldn't be this hard for me to keep my eyes on his face and not on his bare chest. "It's lucky you could fill in for Charlie this year."

"I'm happy to help," Henry replies as he unclips his suspenders.

Fuck, fuck, fuck. I need to get out of here. I also need to get a grip.

I open my mouth, hellbent on offering to leave him in peace to change his shirt, but he continues speaking before I get the chance. "And I'll take any excuse for a couple extra days here. I love Wintermore at Christmas."

My lips twist into a grimace. I try to hide it, but I've never been great at hiding my feelings.

Henry laughs, a deep, rumbly sound I can feel in my toes. "You don't like Wintermore at Christmas?"

"I don't like Christmas, period. And Wintermore is as Christ-massy as it gets."

Henry wrinkles his brow like I've spoken another language as he pulls a crisp white Henley out of his duffel and over his head. Unfortunately for me, he looks no less incredible covered up.

"Everyone likes Christmas. How can you not like Christmas?"

I hardly process the words coming out of his mouth as I watch him shrug on his jacket and buckle the thick black belt that closes it. He doesn't have the hat on yet, thank fucking god.

What is happening to me? What is this? There's not a chance in the world that I'm attracted to this man in a Santa suit.

Henry tilts his head, an amused smile playing around his lips.

Shit, he asked me a question.

"I just don't," I answer, trying my hand at a nonchalant shrug despite my racing heart. Giving him no chance to respond, I shoulder my camera bag and nod to the door. "We should probably get set up in the grotto."

Henry steps back and gestures down the hall. "Lead the way."

I rummage in my camera bag, walking with purpose toward the back of the toy store, and pull out a sour watermelon candy. I unwrap it and sigh when it touches my tongue with a comforting sting.

Noelle is placing some last-minute plastic snowmen along the vinyl path that leads to the grotto. "Perfect, you found each other." Her eyes widen as she takes in my outfit. "Shit. Yeah, I see the problem now. I'll look for a different costume for you. You good to get everything set up?"

I nod, and she claps her hands excitedly, dancing across the store and singing along to the Christmas music.

"I think you look great," Henry says beside me.

I jump. "Huh?"

"Noelle said she sees the problem, but I don't. You look great."

Nothing about the compliment feels sleazy or suggestive, but I can't even begin to process it as I face the entrance to the grotto and see the real problem: Henry and I, inside a dark, ten-by-ten room, alone, while he's dressed like that and I, apparently, am losing my fucking mind.

Fifteen hours across two flights. A two-hour drive to Wintermore.

Eight hours photographing excited, sticky children. Nine hours in the grotto with Henry. It's been a long fucking day.

But not one of those things excuses what I'm about to do.

I swirl the white wine around my glass and narrow my eyes at my laptop. My favorite porn site stares at me from the screen.

Blowing out a breath, I drain the glass.

"Fuck it," I mutter, pulling the laptop closer and typing one word into the search box: *Santa*.

2
HENRY

December 4

This ain't my first Santa rodeo.

Charlie and I grew up in a small town about halfway between Austin and San Antonio, and Addie Creek Santa was a hereditary position. It started with Gramps, then Dad took over when he started having trouble remembering what the kids wanted for Christmas.

Charlie moved to Wintermore before he got the chance to take over from Dad, but I carried on the tradition, going home to Addie Creek every Christmas until Mom passed a couple of years ago. My old high school gym teacher wears the hat now.

Charlie moving here and opening the store meant I hadn't had a Christmas with him, Kate, or the kids in twenty years—long enough that the kids aren't kids anymore. But Mom and Dad had no interest in leaving Texas, and Charlie couldn't leave town at their busiest time of year, so I spent Christmas with them.

Until Mom passed, I didn't even get the chance to visit Wintermore. Which explains why I've never met any of the people I've heard them talking about over the years. One person in particular: Rora.

It's just as well. If she'd been any younger when we met, it would make the way I momentarily forget how to speak every time she looks at me *even more* problematic. I don't know how old she is, but she has to be a similar age to Noelle or Felix.

I've been watching her behind the lens of her camera all

morning. She's dazzling. Her hair is golden blonde and falls past her shoulders, in a messy way that looks intentional. Her green eyes are framed with smudged brown shadow, her cheeks rosy pink and covered in gold shimmer.

She's small. Like, *really* small. I'd be surprised if she were taller than five feet, but she commands the room like the tallest person here. She's wearing that distracting-as-fuck elf costume, but I swear I hardly notice it. I don't want to be creepy and stare at her, but it's hard to look anywhere but at her face when she's so focused on her craft. And on the kids. I'd put money on this not being *her* first Santa rodeo either because Rora is incredible with them. And clearly not a fan of pushy parents.

She crosses her arms, not bothering to hide her glare at the mom fussing with the kid sitting on my lap. He has a spiky faux hawk—the result of bubblegum gone wrong, according to his mom, who's trying desperately to smooth his hair down and button the kid's shirt right up to his neck, even though he's squirming uncomfortably.

"Sit *still*, Benji," she scolds. "Do as you're told, or Santa won't bring you any presents."

I watch as Rora narrows her eyes. "Ma'am, we don't use Santa as a threat here."

The mom turns to face Rora with a pout. *Jesus.* "I just want the pictures to be perfect."

Rora takes a deep breath, as if she's counting to three in her head, before replying. "Surely you'd rather Benji had fun meeting Santa and the pictures looked like your son than a catalog version of him?"

Benji's mom begrudgingly nods.

"Great. Then perhaps you could trust me to do my job and make that happen."

With a resigned sigh, the mom leaves her kid alone and steps back.

Rora turns her attention back to Benji, her energy transforming. She's not smiley. In fact, I don't think I've seen her smile once since we met, but her energy is captivating, and the kids love it; she's bright but deep, intense but fun. Like a song you find stuck in your head at all hours of the day, and you just can't quite put your finger on why it consumes you so much.

She claps her hands together before holding her camera up. "Alright, Benji. You're looking great! You know, faux hawks are all the rage in the North Pole right now. Isn't that right, Santa?"

You'd never know she hated Christmas with how well she pretends for the kids.

"Absolutely. You'd fit right in with the elves," I tell Benji.

His face lights up. "I want to be an elf when I grow up!"

"Benj—" his mom starts.

Rora stops her with one quick raised brow. "What are we thinking, Benji? A big smile?"

She never tells the kids what to do. She asks them. It's not something I've ever really thought about, but it makes the kids more comfortable and less awkward.

Benji nods, his mouth stretching in a toothy grin.

I smile at the camera, and Rora snaps away, crouching down and standing on her tiptoes, testing different angles.

It's a far cry from the Santa pictures I'm used to. Back in Addie Creek, the parents just take their own pictures. My only experience with professional pictures was tagging along when Charlie and Kate took Felix and Noelle to a department store in Austin to get their pictures taken because they weren't fooled by my dad in his Santa suit. Those pictures had been stuffy and formal.

Rora pauses and squints at the little screen on her camera. "Oh wow, you're a natural. Great job!"

She gives me a small nod, a signal that she has what she needs, and I'm up.

"Are you excited for Christmas, Benji?" I ask, and he immediately starts talking a mile a minute, telling me about their Christmas plans.

One thing I already love about being Santa here is how unhurried it is. There's no rush to get as many kids in and out as possible; every kid gets their moment to talk about whatever they want. Rora uses this time to check and quickly edit the pictures, and activities are set up outside the grotto for waiting families. It's a perfect system.

"What would you like for Christmas?"

Benji's mom leans in closer to listen to his answer.

He gives me a serious look. "I want a baby brother or sister."

His mom's face falls.

Shit. "I don't think the elves can make you one of those since Christmas is just in a few weeks," I reply gently, which seems to placate him. "Is there a toy you might like instead?"

"A Bubbles RV *with* the tent. The red one."

I quickly glance over his shoulder, and his mom nods, looking relieved. "I'll certainly see what we can do," I promise, and help him down from my lap. I wish him a Merry Christmas, giving him one of the stockings we hand out to the kids, and Rora directs his mom to the register, where Noelle will help with the pictures.

Rora rolls her neck with a groan when they leave the grotto, glancing at the snowman clock above the entrance. "We should take a five-minute break before the next family. Stretch out, chug some coffee." She grabs the travel coffee cups Noelle gave us this morning from below the desk and hands one to me as I stand up.

We've been stealing sips here and there between families, but this is the first time we've actually stopped to caffeinate. And I desperately need it.

I inhale the peppermint mocha with a happy sigh before stretching my arms above my head and easing some of the tension from my body. The throne isn't uncomfortable, but balancing wriggly kids on my lap is almost as much work as a trip to the gym.

Rora drags her eyes up my form to the tips of my fingers, where they almost graze the ceiling. She looks away quickly when she realizes I've noticed her watching.

"I forget how tall you are until you stand up," she says, focusing on her coffee. "Charlie always complained about his back hurting when he was Santa. It's got to be worse for you."

"I was going to ask if you've done this before, but that answers that," I reply with a chuckle. "You're great with the kids."

"This was my job every Christmas in high school. I might hate Christmas, but I love working with kids." She rubs the back of her neck like it's aching underneath her camera strap.

"Why don't you use a tripod?"

"I've never liked staying still while I work," she explains. "I've always been on the move. My parents are photographers—"

"Wildlife, right?" Charlie and Kate have spoken about Rora and her parents over the years, and I vaguely remember Kate mentioning something about wildlife photography.

Rora looks surprised that I know. "Yeah. Well, my mom's a wildlife photographer. My dad's a landscape photographer. Both specialties require a lot of patience. When I was young, they placed a bet on which of them I would take after, but they very quickly realized I didn't have the patience for either."

One of the guys on my research base is a hobby photographer and once told me he spent six hours lying still trying to photograph a rare migrating bird. Just a couple of days of watching Rora work, and I can't imagine her staying still for half of that.

"How did you land on photojournalism?" I ask, clinging to the little pieces of her I'm getting to know. I've picked things up here and there through my family, but I like hearing her talk.

"I've had a camera in my hand since I could walk, and I just kind of fell into it naturally," she answers with a shrug. "I was always looking for interesting stories through the lens. My parents recognized what I was doing and guided me in the right direction. How did you get into climatology?"

I'm not sure anyone's asked me that since college, when my fellow students and I were still full of hope that we were going to make a difference.

"There was a heat wave in '88. It was all over the news, and I was fascinated, but trying to get any information on why it was happening was nearly impossible in Texas. I got my fair share of lectures on 'questioning God's will' when I asked. My parents weren't religious and found a few books for me. I had nightmares about climate change for a month, then woke up one morning and told anyone who would listen that I was going to fix it."

"That's adorable," Rora replies, her eyes twinkling. "How is fixing it going?"

I snort. "Not well."

"I figured. Do you at least still like your job?"

I sit back down on the throne to finish my coffee, and Rora perches on the stool that's off to the side for families. "It's complicated. I like my job, yeah, but I've also been doing the same thing for a decade now and I'm a little bored. I'm in the highest role at the station. There's no way of moving up unless I'm willing to travel."

"You don't want to travel? It's the best," Rora says, and I can see on her face how much she loves it. There's a hunger there, like she can't wait to get back out on the road.

"I like traveling. It's just… I got a job offer, actually, just before I came here. It's a more senior position where I'd be traveling to different stations and visiting various research labs, liaising between research teams, auditing setups and research, overseeing training… That kind of thing. But I haven't decided if I'm taking it yet."

Rora stares at me, open-mouthed. "Why wouldn't you take it? That sounds amazing and exactly what you need if you're bored." She's the first person, aside from my boss, to see it that way.

My team in Greenland doesn't want me to leave, and my family would rather I found something closer to Wyoming than accept a job that will take me all over the world.

"It does sound amazing," I agree. "But I don't know. I think I might be too old to start over like that." Not to mention the niggling worry that it's not my current job role that's boring me but my entire career.

She rolls her eyes. "Come *on.* You're not old." Her gaze snags on something, and she leans forward, reaching toward my hat. "Stay still a sec."

I do as she says, holding my breath as I feel the heat of her skin near my face. Her fingers are gentle, tugging something from the edge of my hat.

She pulls back a little, showing me the shiny purple piece of foil. "Tinsel." Her voice is hushed, her eyes wide like she's just realized how close we are. She swallows, sitting back, a soft flush on her face. "So, how old are you?" The question feels weighted, like it has less to do with our previous conversation than it would have a second ago.

"Forty-seven."

She breathes out deeply, surprise flickering in her eyes. "That's not old."

Did she expect me to be younger? Older?

She takes my empty coffee cup from the floor beside the throne and stashes it with hers below the desk before heading for the entrance to the grotto to let the next family in.

"How old are you?" The question slips out before I can stop it.

She looks over her shoulder at me, running her tongue along her lower lip before answering. "I'm twenty-eight." She steps out of the grotto, and I lean my head back against the throne with a heavy sigh.

She's twenty-eight.

Fuck.

3
RORA

December 5

Someone's in my house. I rub my face and open my eyes, squinting at the daylight and groaning at the soft sounds of banging and jingling coming from downstairs.

That better be Noelle. I refuse to be murdered in Wintermore at Christmas.

Forcing myself out of bed, I pull a blanket around my shoulders and shove my feet in slippers before trudging downstairs.

Technically, this is my parents' house, but I'm not in Wintermore enough to get my own place. Hell, my parents aren't in Wintermore enough to hang on to such a big house, but apartments in town hardly ever come up. Noelle and Felix still live at home because it's easier than fighting for one of the few apartments. And this house is just across the street, so they can get away if they ever need a little space.

I yawn as I walk into the living room. Sure enough, my best friend is standing in the center of the room, with her hair piled on top of her head in a messy bun. It's a medium-warm brown these days, as close to her natural color as I've seen in a while, but the ends are still slightly blue-tinged from her last color experiment.

She's holding something behind her back with a guilty expression, as if I can't see the boxes of Christmas decorations dotted around the room.

"It's too early for this."

"It's December fifth," she protests, brandishing a silver moon ornament from behind her back. "We've had our tree up for weeks."

"I meant too early in the morning."

"Ah. I can help with that." Noelle spins around, and she has a takeout coffee cup in hand when she turns back.

I can smell the caffeine from across the room. Heavenly. "Gimme." I grab the cup and fall ungracefully onto the couch, breathing in the sweet vanilla syrup and coconut milk—my favorite. "This is good. Thank you."

"You're welcome. Oh, my parents want you to come over for brunch when we're finished decorating, by the way."

"That sounds perfect." The brunch, not the decorating. "Why are you decorating my living room before dawn?" I ask once I've had a few sips of the latte.

Monday is the only day the store is closed; you'd think she'd want to sleep in.

"It's 10:30. You must have been having some pretty sweet dreams to sleep this long. Anything good?"

"Oh, I don't remember." I do, but it's probably best not to mention who I was dreaming about. I clear my throat. "The 'why are you decorating' part still stands."

"You know the rules," she says, turning her attention back to the boxes and pulling out an artificial Christmas tree.

Great.

"You mean the rule that all houses in Wintermore need to be decorated *outside*? I already have lights outside. You put them up years ago, and they're on a timer." I'm pretty sure the town couldn't actually do anything if I didn't have the lights up, but I'm never usually here for Christmas, so it doesn't affect me either way. Most houses here leave lights up year-round.

"Felix put them up, actually. That's why they're crooked," Noelle says, and I think it's safe to assume I'm not getting an answer to why she's decorating *inside*.

She loves decorating, so if it makes her happy, she can turn this place into the North Pole. I grew up with the Whittens; I'm used to blocking out Christmas decorations.

I jump as Noelle tosses a crinkly paper bag at me. "That's for you."

Green velvet greets me as I peek inside, and I pull out a new skirt for my elf costume. It looks at least a couple of inches longer, and it has pockets.

"For your candy," Noelle says when I excitedly point them out. "There's some in the bag."

I'm already tearing into the bag before she's finished talking, tossing a blue raspberry-flavored sour candy into my tongue and sighing happily. Better than caffeine. "You want one?"

"No, thanks. I value my tastebuds too much."

My obsession with sour candy started when I was nine. I had the worst case of strep I'd ever had and almost completely lost my taste. The only things I enjoyed were sour: candy, pickles, straight lemons, and limes. Have I fucked up my tastebuds over the years so I find most foods bland now? Maybe, but I travel enough that I can always find something extra flavorful.

"So," Noelle begins, sounding entirely too nonchalant for my liking. "You going to tell me yet why you got fired?"

"There's really not much to tell. I had a press pass for a political gala in London, but they took it back last minute. Apparently, the politician who was the guest of honor disagrees with the concept of female journalists. I snuck in, and I got caught. That's it."

I made it in and out without an issue, so sure I'd gotten away with it. My boss loved the pictures and was happy to print them anonymously, but it turned out *her* boss was friendly with the politician and didn't want to risk burning bridges by printing them. Or by keeping me on staff, apparently.

"Assholes," Noelle growls. "You worked there for six years, and they fired you for one mistake? After all the incredible work you did for them? It's their loss."

"I was tired of working on soulless assignments, anyway. There was no art in it anymore. I've been thinking about leaving and going freelance for a while. This is just the push I needed." I grab another blanket from the back of the couch and toss it over myself as I tell Noelle about my plans to take a month or so off before picking up freelance work.

Getting fired isn't great for my reputation, but I have enough friends in the industry to vouch for me. And thanks to them, I had multiple freelance agencies in my email inbox within days of losing my job. It's going to take time to build up a maintainable freelance career, but it's doable. I just need a break first.

"What about you? Any further along with the bakery plans?"

"No," Noelle replies, sounding more dejected than she looks, angrily stringing lights on the tree branches. "Hard to make plans to leave the store when I can't trust Felix to do his job. And now that everyone in town is obsessed with Shay Harland's place, there's probably no point in me opening a bakery."

Noelle has dreamed of owning a year-round Christmas-themed bakery since the Whittens moved to Wintermore. There's only one other bakery in town, a fancy patisserie-style café run by Shay Harland—Noelle's mortal enemy, even though she doesn't know it. I like Shay—not that I'd ever admit it—and she's an incredible baker, but Noelle makes magic in the kitchen, and I know a Christmas-themed bakery would go down a treat in Wintermore.

"*Épices et Sucré*. What does that even mean?" she scoffs.

"It means Spicy and Sweet," I reply automatically, and Noelle glares at me. "There's space for two bakeries in a town that likes treats so much. And everyone here loves you. They'll support you. Do you want me to talk to Felix about getting his shit together?"

Noelle shakes her head, grabbing ornaments from a box and hanging them on the tree. "There's no point." She adds a silver

Sophie Snow

star to the top of the tree and crouches down to plug the lights in before stepping back to admire her work. "What do you think?"

It *is* a Christmas tree, so it's never going to be my dream decor, but Noelle has done a beautiful job. The lights are a pretty gradient of aurora colors, and there are just a few stars and moons dangling from the tree. By Whitten tree standards, it's practically bare, but I appreciate her not going overboard.

"It's gorgeous, as always."

Noelle drops onto the couch beside me with a satisfied smile. "Thanks for letting me put it up. I owe you—more than I already owed you for saving my ass with the Santa pictures, anyway."

"You don't owe me," I reply, rolling my eyes and nudging her with my shoulder.

She yawns and turns to face me, purple smudges below her gray-blue eyes. We're only a few days into December, and the hoards of holiday tourists are already taking their toll. I know Noelle wouldn't change it, though; she lives for this time of year.

"What do you want for Christmas? You're getting an extra special present for coming home this year."

I open my mouth to protest but close it before anything spills out. There's only one *want* on my list right now, and asking Noelle would be wholly inappropriate.

But she did say she owes me. What's the harm in asking?

"I'd like permission to seduce your uncle, please."

Noelle blinks three times in quick succession. "My uncle Henry?"

"Do you have another uncle I've never heard of?"

She raises a brow. "Why? Do you want to weigh up your options? Wait, sorry. That was bitchy. I've been watching a lot of *Real Housewives* lately. Okay. To be clear, for Christmas, you want my permission to have sex with my uncle Henry?"

When you put it like that… I've already put it out there. Might as well keep going.

"Yes, please."

Noelle purses her lips, her eyebrows drawing together in thought. I almost tell her to forget I said anything, but she finally sighs and says, "I can't wrap that. But you should. You getting knocked up by my uncle would make Christmas pretty awkward."

"Is that a yes?"

Her phone vibrates, and she glances at it. "Brunch is ready." She stands up, but I give her an expectant look. "Fine. It's a yes, but you still need to give me a Christmas list so I can actually buy you something."

I jump up and pull her into a hug. "You're the best best friend ever."

I have no idea why she brought so many boxes of decor for such a minimal tree, but I throw on some warm clothes and help her carry them across the street.

"I don't understand *why* you want him," Noelle says, wrinkling her nose.

"I wouldn't expect you to, considering you're related to him."

"True, but he's old."

"He's only forty-seven."

"Right. Old." The Whitten's porch steps creak under our snow boots. "Do you have a plan to, you know, *seduce him*?" She waggles her eyebrows.

"I haven't really thought about it yet. I didn't think it was an option ten minutes ago."

Of course, there's more than Noelle to think about, but she sees us every day at work, and she's uncannily observant. She'd probably notice if we tried to keep it from her. The rest of the Whittens never need to know.

"I might have an idea," Noelle says, pushing open the door with her shoulder and walking straight into her mom.

"An idea for what, honey?"

We exchange a wide-eyed look. "Um, we were just talking about organizing the back room at the store a little better," I say.

Kate doesn't question the flimsy answer. "That's a great idea!"

Later, Noelle mouths at me as we close the door behind us.

We drop the boxes at the bottom of the stairs, and I give Kate, Charlie, and Felix good morning hugs before taking my usual seat at the dining table.

"Where's Uncle Henry?" Noelle asks through a mouthful of pancake.

"At the gym," Charlie says, piling breakfast potatoes onto his plate.

Visions of Henry working out fill my head, and I have to force myself to focus on the conversation as Charlie asks me how my parents are.

"I texted your dad a couple of weeks ago, but I haven't heard back. I'm guessing he's somewhere remote taking pictures?"

"They're in the Amazon for six weeks," I explain, not remotely surprised that my parents forgot to tell Charlie and Kate, aka their best friends, that they were planning to drop off the face of the planet for almost two months. We talk all the time when we all have phone service, and sometimes they still forget to tell me where they're going.

My parents and Charlie and Kate were best friends as fast as Noelle and I were, more like family than anything else. The Whittens moved to Wintermore when I was seven, at the height of the Christmas movie popularity, right as things started to fall apart in my family. It would've been easy for my parents to resent them, to brush them off as part of the festive problem, but it really was love at first sight between the Stanleys and the Whittens. Within a couple of months, it was like we'd known each other forever, and suddenly, I had not one but two sets of incredible parents in my life.

I love my mom and dad, but they never wanted to be tied down here, and our relationship only got better when the Whittens were happy to look after me so they could travel for work. Their relationship, on the other hand, not so much.

"They're planning to come back to the US after Brazil," I continue. "I'm sure they'll stop here for a while."

"Wait, they're in the Amazon *together?*" Kate asks, exchanging a surprised look with Charlie.

"Mm-hmm. They still think it's a secret that they're together again."

"They have to tell us eventually. It's been years," Felix says, and we all agree.

We've long suspected my parents have been seeing each other again, and I don't know why they're being so cagey about it, but they'll tell us when they're ready.

"I hope we can all get together sometime next year. It's been too long. Maybe a weekend at the cabin," Charlie suggests.

I hardly hear a word he says because the front door opens, and Henry walks in, wearing nothing but a gray skin-tight t-shirt and workout shorts. In this weather. *Fuck.*

His cheeks are red, his hair slicked back, and it's far too early in the morning for me to be thinking about licking the sweat from—

"*Ow.*"

"Stop drooling," Noelle hisses out of the corner of her mouth, elbowing me once more for good measure.

Henry says hello but pauses at my chair, smiling down. "Mornin'."

"Morning," I reply, trying not to stare at the outline of his pecs through his t-shirt. "Good workout?"

"Tiring. There was a group of old ladies who were definitely outrunning me on the treadmills, and I stupidly tried to keep up."

"That'll be Agnes Lemon and her knitting group," Kate tells him, and I breathe a small sigh of relief when he turns his bright blue eyes to her. "Go get cleaned up and come grab some food. There's plenty to go around."

Henry stretches before heading toward the stairs. "Sounds good. I'm starving."

He gives me one last passing smile, and I pick up my coffee just to give my hands something to do.

This man.

4
HENRY
December 6

S oft, folky pop music plays through the store's speakers as I close the door and call Rora's name.

"In the grotto," she shouts back, and even from the front door, I can hear her grumbling something that sounds a lot like, "Fucking Christmas," under her breath.

When Noelle suggested we do this, I thought she was fucking with us. I'm pretty sure Charlie never had to pose for sexy Santa pictures to advertise the store's Santa After Dark party—a night the store stays open late for adults to shop without kids around, with cocktails, canapés, and a Santa photo booth.

I trust Noelle's business sense—the store is thriving under her —but I'm not sold on this idea. And although she didn't complain, I can't imagine Rora is. Why would she be? She's a serious journalist who's stuck in a town she hates, taking pictures for a holiday she hates. I'm sure the last thing she wants to be doing is spending more time taking Christmas pictures, especially *sexy* pictures of a man almost twenty years older than her.

Rora is in the grotto, standing on her tiptoes on the throne, sans shoes, hanging lights on the wall. Or trying to. She can't be taller than five feet, teetering on the plush velvet seat.

"Can I help?" I ask, dropping my bag by the door and watching her hopping warily. It's so precarious that I almost manage to keep my eyes off the skintight leggings hugging her ass.

"I've got it." The lights slip through her fingers, and she grabs them just before they fall out of reach.

"You sure?"

Her head whips around, icy fire in her eyes.

I hold my hands up. "You're right. You've got it. I don't know what I was thinking."

Except she doesn't have it. After two almost-falls, she drops the lights, and a curse spills from her lips. It takes everything in me not to laugh because god knows she'd be pissed.

I grab the lights and ignore her outstretched hand. "Please let me help, sugar."

Her eyes widen almost imperceptibly for a second before she narrows them. "Does that work for you?"

"What?"

"Saying 'sugar' in that Texas drawl of yours to get people to do what you want."

"Usually." I don't mention that I have no idea where "sugar" came from. I'm not one for nicknames, but the accent usually does the trick alone.

Rora sighs, but I swear her eyes darken, her pupils swallowing her hazy green irises. "I can see how it would work."

She lets me help her down from the throne, her hand soft in mine. I don't want to let her go, but I have no excuse to hold her hand when her feet are flat on the ground again.

I turn away and hang the lights on the hooks with ease.

"Showoff. I could've done it. I'm five-three, you know," Rora mutters, but my answering laugh dies when I turn back to find her tugging her crewneck over her head. She's not wearing a t-shirt, just a light blue racerback sports bra that matches the stripes up the sides of her leggings.

My gaze sticks to the tattoo I noticed on the day we met when I was trying not to stare at her in that red bra: three pine trees, a small cabin, and a swirl of the aurora borealis disappearing below the band. It's beautiful.

Rora notices my gaze, and my cheeks warm.

"Have you seen them?" I ask, nodding at the ink. There's no point in pretending I wasn't staring.

"The auroras?" she asks, and I nod. "Nope. Ironic, considering I was named after them. My parents met in Norway, photographing the Northern Lights. The company they booked their cabins with double-booked them, and nine months later, I came along. I'll catch them one day."

"That's quite the meet-cute. Do they still live in town?" I ask, lifting my bag onto the throne and rummaging for my suit. I know better than to stuff it in a bag, given how easily velvet creases, but I didn't want to wear it on the walk to the store and risk running into a kid.

"This is technically their home address," Rora says, hanging her camera around her neck and taking a couple of shots, testing the lighting, I assume. "They both travel for work and don't come back often. They like Wintermore even less than I do."

"Damn. Poor Wintermore." I look from the Santa suit in my hand to Rora. "You know, if you're not comfortable with this, we don't have to do it. We can say no."

"With the shoot?" Rora asks, confusion filling her eyes when I nod. "Why would I be uncomfortable?"

"Uh, you know." I toy with the edge of my belt. It needs polishing, but I like the scuffs and cracks in the leather. They give it character. "Sexy photoshoots aren't exactly your thing, and I'm older and—"

Rora's eyes widen, and she holds up a hand. "Oh, I'm with you. Seriously, I don't mind at all. I know I don't have any reason to feel uncomfortable with you. Are you okay with it? You can say no, too."

"If it'll help the store, I'm up for it. I'm just going to change outside." I hold up the clothes and head for the curtain, but Rora stops me, a hand on the fabric.

"Would you be comfortable leaving the shirt off? And the

beard and wig. So, just the hat, pants, belt, suspenders, and open jacket?" Her hair is falling across her face, but I can still see the blush on her cheeks.

"Sure," I agree, and because I apparently have no fucking filter, I add, "Nothing you haven't seen before."

I don't give her a chance to respond, mentally kicking myself as I step out of the grotto, pull the curtain closed, and take a deep breath. What the fuck is wrong with me?

"I know I don't have any reason to feel uncomfortable with you."

Would Rora say that if she knew the thoughts running through my mind every time I look at her? The filthy fantasies playing like a film reel I can't escape every time I close my eyes? Definitely not.

The last thing I want is for her to feel uncomfortable around me, which means I have to keep my thoughts to myself and she can never know.

Unzipping my jeans, I grasp at a subject change. "Do you see your parents often?"

"We only see each other a few times a year, but we talk all the time when they have service. They go to some pretty remote places."

"You must miss them." I know how hard being away from family can be, but at least mine were always reachable by phone when I was in Greenland.

"I do, but we're all happier doing what we love. And it makes the time we spend together more—" She looks up as I pull back the curtain, and I still as she takes me in, her eyes glazing over. Her expression... Fuck, I don't know what to do with that.

I clear my throat. "More?"

Rora flicks her eyes up to mine. "Um, more? You look great as is."

This flustered version of Rora reminds me of how she was on the morning we met. How we both were.

"Your parents. It makes the time you spend together more…"

Realization dawns on Rora's face. "Right. It makes it more special. Anyway, should we get started?"

She turns away as I head for the throne, but not before I see her close her eyes and blow out a breath. Her camera beeps when she turns it on, slinging the strap over her neck. She squints down at the screen, holding the camera up to check the lighting.

"Perfect," she murmurs before looking up at me. "Ready?"

It isn't until I open my mouth to respond that nerves roll over me. "Uh… I have no idea how to do this."

"How to do what?" Rora asks, lowering her camera and stepping closer to me.

One step, two, and the racing in my chest suddenly has less to do with my nerves.

"The 'sexy Santa' thing."

Rora narrows her eyes, considering me. She runs her tongue along the edge of her teeth before saying, "Henry. You *are* the 'sexy Santa' thing. You don't have to do anything."

Oh. I have no idea how to respond to that. Not in a way that's remotely appropriate. "Should I pose or something?" I might not address what she says directly, but the words come out breathy enough to address it for me.

"Just look at the camera like it's someone you"—Rora holds the camera up, peering at me over it—"want to put on the naughty list."

Jesus fucking Christ.

It's easy to think of Rora when I look into the lens; she's standing right there. Close enough that I can smell the sweet coconut scent that follows her around, haunting me every time she comes near me.

I should feel guilty—I *do* feel guilty—for thinking of her, but she voices her approval, snapping away.

"Why do you hate Christmas so much?" I ask when she pauses to flick through the pictures she's taken.

"It's stupid," she replies, shaking her head. "My parents blamed Christmas for their divorce, which means I also blamed Christmas for their divorce."

That's not what I expected. "Was it to blame?"

She shrugs. "Indirectly. I told you my mom got pregnant the night they met, right? They got married two weeks later and picked Wintermore to settle down in because the mountains were good for both of them, photography-wise. Back then, they were practically untouched. When Wintermore became the Christmas capital of America, not so much. After all the hotels, ski lodges, and tourist places showed up and it became so busy with tourists, my parents couldn't work here anymore. They hated it. So, they took turns traveling while the other stayed home with me, and all it did was make them resent each other."

"Shit, I'm sorry."

Rora waves my apology away. "It's fine, honestly. They got married way too soon, way too young, and it was always going to end in divorce. It was best for everyone."

Any time I've heard Rora speak about her parents, there's been no resentment in her voice. Surprising, considering how most people would react to something as magical as Christmas being ruined for them.

"Are they on good terms now?"

"Oh, yeah. They've been secretly seeing each other again for years. They'll admit it one day."

Talk about a non-traditional family dynamic. "Surely, if they're back together now, you don't have to hate Christmas so much," I point, and Rora rolls her eyes.

"Nice try." She holds her camera back up, and I focus on the lens again. "You can still talk. We want them to feel natural."

Talking while she's taking pictures feels anything but natural, but she's the professional. "This shoot has to be your ideal of hell."

"How so?"

"I can't imagine anything is less sexy for you than Santa."

She's quiet for a moment, the click of her camera the only sound, before answering, "You know, I kind of get it. The Santa thing."

At first, I think I've misheard her. I forget all about the camera, my jaw dropping as I stare at her. "Seriously? You?"

"I can't say the shocked expression is working for the pictures," she says with a chuckle, and I close my mouth. Her eyes are blazing, her pupils dilated, her face flushed. "But yeah, I get it. The suit, the power, the 'he sees you when you're sleeping' thing. There's something kind of hot about the thought of Santa just sitting by the fire, watching you sleep, deciding if you're naughty or nice."

Her low voice coils through me, warming my blood, and sending every drop of that blood directly to my cock. *Fuck.* I shift. *How obvious would it be if I clasped my hands in my lap*? Probably not as obvious as how fucking hard I am, which Rora will almost definitely notice when she's editing the pictures.

It's a lose-lose situation.

I sit forward so my jacket covers my lap a bit. "I can see how that would be…" It isn't until I'm speaking that I really let myself think about the fantasy Rora mentioned, and my jacket is no longer doing anything to help. Shit. I know exactly what I'm going to be thinking about when I'm struggling to fall asleep later.

I swallow, my skin tingling. "I get it."

Rora unwinds the camera from her neck and cradles it against her chest, her tongue darting out to lick her bottom lip as she takes me in. "I think I have all the pictures I need."

"Great."

She turns away, and I rub my face with my hands. Was I imagining it, or was she … flirting? It's probably just because we're stuck in this tiny room together all day, every day, and Rora apparently has a Santa fantasy. *It has nothing to do with you at all. You just happen to be here*, I tell myself as I sit back.

Rora crouches by our bags, packing her camera stuff. "Do you want a ride?"

"I— What?" I ask, my eyes widening as she stretches to pull her sweater over her head.

"You walked here, right? I have my car."

God, I need to get a grip. "Right, yeah. I'm good, thanks. I didn't make it to the gym today, so I should probably walk." And I absolutely can't get up from this throne while she's in the room. "I'm going to change before I head out in case I run into any kids, so I can lock up."

"Sounds good. Goodnight."

"Sweet dreams, sugar."

"Thanks, you too." The corner of her mouth lifts almost imperceptibly. It's the closest I've seen to a smile on her lips since we met, though she smiles with her beautiful eyes constantly.

When I hear the front door close, I stand up. I shed the suit and set my bag on the throne to grab my outside clothes, but my fingers freeze as they graze the white Henley. There's a folded piece of paper sitting on top that wasn't there when I changed into the suit. Only Rora could have put it there.

Curiosity gets the better of me, and I tear into the note like a kid on Christmas morning. My eyes scan her neat, loopy script three times before the words sink in.

I suck in a breath, pushing my bag from the throne and sitting, stunned. I almost crush the note in my fist, but I don't want to wrinkle it.

I swallow and read it once more, my mind already half made up.

I'm usually asleep by midnight, and there's a spare key under the blue plant pot by the door if you're interested. If you're not, let's not make it weird tomorrow.

Rora

P.S. Wear the Santa suit.

P.P.S. My safe word is candy cane.

5
HENRY

December 7

I look at the note in my palm, then away. And back, and away, and rinse and repeat, no less than a dozen times. It's a quarter after midnight. I'm wearing the suit. That's pretty much confirmation that I'm going, but I can't make my feet move. On the scale of good to bad ideas, sneaking out to hook up with my niece's twenty-eight-year-old best friend falls firmly on the bad idea side. I pinch the spot between my brows and groan.

If you're interested.

Of course, I'm fucking interested. I've been interested since the second Rora's eyes met mine. One look at her mossy green eyes, and I forgot we were both standing half naked in the back room of my brother's toy store. It would be so easy to lose myself in the depths of her. I haven't stopped imagining sinking my fingers into her hair since that day, but I never imagined she might be interested back. I'm almost twenty years older than her. Jesus.

What are the odds that the biggest Christmas hater I've ever met has a goddamn Santa kink?

I fold the note and tuck it in my wallet, making a mental pros and cons list. Cons: she's twenty-eight, we work together, and she's practically family. Pros: I really fucking want to.

My mind was made up the second I put on the suit; there's no point in pretending I have enough self-control to pay attention to any of the cons.

You'd think, at forty-seven, I'd be less nervous to sneak out of my brother's house, but I tiptoe down the stairs like I might be caught doing something wrong. Which is ridiculous. It's not sneaking out. I'm an adult, and I'm allowed to leave the house after dark to partake in adult activities. Even if said adult activities involve someone my brother views as a bonus kid. But I'm just not going to think about that.

I carefully push the kitchen door open and stop as Noelle looks up from a bar stool at the island, a chocolate croissant between her teeth. She gives me a once-over and narrows her eyes.

"Hey, you're up late," I say, closing the door behind me. Apparently, I did need to sneak out. "I'm just—"

She holds up a hand. "I know what you're doing, and I don't need to hear about it." The croissant muffles her words.

She knows? I don't know if that's better or worse, but I'm leaning toward worse. What the fuck am I doing? I should just go back upstairs and forget this ever happened.

Noelle drops the remains of her croissant on the island with a sigh and brushes crumbs from her *Elf* sleep shirt. "I can tell you're spiraling. Look, Rora asked me to make sure I was cool with it before she made her move, or whatever, and I am." She screws up her face. "Actually, I'm decidedly less cool with it now that I know what you're wearing, but, like I said, I don't need to hear about it. Go, have a good night, and let's never ever talk about it."

If Rora asked Noelle, that means it wasn't a split-second decision. She's been thinking about this. Knowing that helps me drag my feet through the doubt and out of the door, wishing Noelle a good night as I go.

I cross the quiet street to Rora's family home, a twenty-second walk from my brother's front door. No wonder she and Noelle were so close growing up. They were literally close. The front of Rora's place is covered in unlit Christmas lights, and a family of smiling snowmen is dotted around the yard. I don't need to question who decorated; it certainly wasn't Rora.

The blue plant pot is where she promised it would be, a small silver key tucked underneath. I slide it into the lock and pause, leaning against the front door.

Am I seriously doing this?

I'm no stranger to casual sex, but I'm used to meeting people in bars or hotels when I travel for work. As much as I can, I avoid hooking up with people working at the research site, definitely none of the other permanent base staff, and I avoid any of the visiting researchers I'm likely to run into again. It's easier to keep things casual if you're not linked to the person you're hooking up with in some way, and there's no doubt I'm inextricably linked to Rora.

That we haven't crossed paths until now is luck—good or bad, I'm not sure yet. But there'll be non-Christmas family events in the future that we'll inevitably both end up attending. Not to mention the next couple of weeks working in the store. It's messy and reckless, and I'm old enough to know better.

But so is Rora. I might be toiling over our age difference, but she's twenty-eight. She's an adult. She knows what she wants, and if my age doesn't bother her, why should it bother me? I have to stop beating myself up for wanting her and give her some damn credit.

I turn the key.

The house is quiet, cast in eerie shadows from the silvery glow of the full moon. I peer up the stairs, wondering where Rora's room is, but cool lights twinkling in the corner of the room catch my eye. They illuminate a sparsely decorated tree with just a few silver stars and moons hanging from the branches. The lights do the heavy lifting: a subtle gradient of blue, green, and purple, like the aurora borealis. Noelle's handiwork, I assume.

Next to her namesake-inspired tree, Rora is fast asleep on the couch. I move slowly across the room, sink into the armchair opposite her, and just take her in.

She has her knees tucked against her chest, her face resting on her hand as she leans over the arm of the couch. Her blonde hair fans over the gray fabric, glowing under the tree lights. She's wearing a surprisingly festive, oversized red and green plaid shirt. A fluffy white blanket covers her legs, but as I watch, she sighs in her sleep and pulls her legs closer to her chest, causing the blanket to slip off, revealing an expanse of goosebump-covered thigh and a sliver of underwear. *Red, again.*

My heart hammers against my ribcage, and I lean forward, elbows on my knees, itching to touch her. I resist, forcing myself to look but not touch. This is all part of what she wanted, after all.

'*He sees you when you're sleeping.*'

God knows I get it now. There's something illicit about sitting here in the hush of Rora's house before she has any idea I'm here, knowing where this night is heading.

My gaze falls to the coffee table, and I have to fight back a laugh at the two fingers of scotch and a plate filled with red and white macarons. I shake my head, lift the scotch to my lips, and sip. It beats milk and cookies, that's for sure.

I shift my weight, and the chair creaks almost imperceptibly, but it's enough. Rora's breathing changes, her body tensing, but her eyes stay closed. I'm about to speak up and reassure her it's just me when she opens her mouth.

"What's the verdict?"

Fucking hell. Her voice—deep, breathy, and still scratchy with sleep—goes straight to my cock.

"The verdict?"

"Naughty or nice?" Her eyes flutter open, reflecting the tree lights like two tiny auroras.

"I'm still deciding," I reply, my voice gruff. "It's a big decision. I need to make sure I get it right."

She hums, sitting up and rolling her neck. The blanket falls to the floor when she stands, her eyes boring into my soul as she crosses the room. "Well, if there's anything I can do to help make up your mind…"

She straddles my lap, and I think I stop breathing, so intimately aware of every spot her body touches mine. The plaid shirt rides up around her thighs, leaving only her underwear and my pants between us. I rest a shaking hand on her back to steady her.

"Hi," she whispers.

"Hi."

"You came."

"I did."

She runs her tongue over her bottom lip. "You freaking out a little?"

I swallow, and Rora's gaze falls to my throat, her pupils dilating. "How could you tell?"

She laughs, a low throaty sound, and snags the glass from my hand. "I figured you might be. Hence the scotch." She brings it to her mouth, taking a swig before pressing the glass back into my hand.

She seems entirely comfortable in my lap, like there's nothing untoward about the fact I'm her best friend's uncle and almost two decades her senior. Her steadiness unties some of the knots in my chest, her smoldering eyes stealing the anxious tension from my body, leaving behind nothing but desperate anticipation. I'm fucking aching for her.

I reach up and set the glass on the mantle without drinking. Rora raises a brow curiously.

I cup her face, brushing my thumb across her soft cheek. She gasps, her thighs tightening around my lap.

"I don't want to be anything less than clear-headed tonight, sugar. I want to remember every millisecond of this."

6
RORA
December 7

Henry's fingers curl around my chin, tugging my face to his. I have a split second to breathe in the sweet candy cane scent that usually has me rolling my eyes before his mouth is on mine. He slips his tongue between my lips, and I groan as I taste him: peppermint with a hint of scotch.

I can't even wrap my head around the fact we're doing this. I'm here, in Wintermore, with Noelle's uncle's tongue in my mouth. He's dressed like fucking Santa Claus, and it's the hottest thing I've ever done in my life.

Only a tiny part of me believed he'd take me up on my offer when I left the note. I hoped I hadn't imagined him flirting while taking his picture, that I hadn't imagined the goosebumps pebbling over his skin when my gaze brushed his chest. I know I didn't imagine the way his pupils flared when I mentioned my Santa fantasy. And it's just as well; though I promised not to make it weird if he wasn't interested, I'm not sure how I would've gone from "hey, I like the idea of Santa watching me sleep" to taking pictures of said Santa tomorrow morning without making it weird.

But now that it's happening, it feels anything but weird. Henry's tongue is unrelenting, meeting mine in desperate strokes that have my heart racing. He loosens his grip on my face, slowly dragging his hands down my back until he has a hold on my waist. He lifts me, shifting my body until I'm straddling just one of his thighs. I cry out, sparks sizzling over my skin as his thigh presses between my legs.

"God," I whimper against his lips.

Henry chuckles, his soft beard and mustache tickling my sensitive skin. "Santa's just fine, baby."

Holy shit. "Santa," I whisper, and Henry groans.

He holds me in a vise grip and slowly rolls my hips. Holy fucking friction. Time slows, and my heart speeds as he grinds my body against his thigh. I feel it everywhere, tingling all the way to my toes.

Admittedly, it's been a while since I hooked up with anyone, but not long enough for how quickly I feel myself spiraling toward an orgasm before I've even taken my underwear off. It's not like I haven't treated myself to an orgasm every night before bed since I met Henry. Thoughts of him have been getting me there since before he stepped foot in this house. I don't even need him guiding my hips anymore; my body has been desperate for this all week.

Henry drags his lips from mine, peppering messy kisses across my jaw and down my throat, before pulling back to look at me. "Fuck, you're so pretty like this, Rora. You're always fucking beautiful, but right now … you're perfect."

He releases my hips, and I still as he brings his fingers to my shirt, hesitating at the buttons.

"Is this okay?"

I nod, not sure I can trust myself to speak.

Henry undoes the top two buttons of the shirt as easily as he's making me come undone, then pauses. "You better keep riding me, sugar. I haven't had nearly enough of those filthy words spilling out of your lips. I'm not sure I've ever seen such a pretty mouth cursing so much."

I do as I'm told, whimpering the very second I start moving again. In my defense, I'm not entirely in control of what's coming out of my mouth right now—a fact I demonstrate when Henry continues unbuttoning my shirt, his fingers taking the first opportunity they get to dance over my red lace bra.

His eyes flame when he recognizes it as the same one I was wearing when we met. "Did you wear this for me?"

"You did such a good job of pretending not to look last time. I figured I'd give you the chance to look as much as you wanted."

He pushes the shirt back until it slips off my shoulders. The cold air hits my skin, but it warms immediately as Henry runs a finger over my collarbone. "Just look?"

"I hope not."

The words have barely left my tongue before he has his hands on me, a guttural groan falling from his mouth as he cups my breasts. He teases my nipples with his thumbs, and my head falls back, sparkles creeping over my vision. With my head back, my chest is pushed closer to Henry, and he wastes no time bending his head and running his tongue over the lace covering my nipples. Even with a barrier between us, it feels incredible.

My nails dig into his shoulders as I hold on tight, riding his thigh closer and closer to the finish line. If I'm not careful, I'm actually going to come all over him.

I slow down, and Henry looks up at me, his expression etched with desire. "You alright?"

"I'm going to…" I trail off, panting. Every word is a goddamn struggle. My head is spinning; my heart is racing. "Fuck. Your pants, I—"

"Oh, sugar," Henry says, grasping my chin between his thumb and forefinger. "You worried you're going to make a mess of the suit?"

I nod, drawing my bottom lip between my teeth.

He leans in closer, stealing it with his own teeth and biting gently before pulling back. I watch, my blood thrumming, as he slips his hands between us. "Sit up a little for me."

When I do, Henry presses the flat of his thumb over my underwear right against my clit.

Fuck, fuck, fuck.

I cry out, struggling to hold myself up as pleasure zips through me. But he doesn't stop there. He removes his thumb and hooks a finger in one side of my underwear, tugging it roughly to the side until the only thing between us is an inch of air and his red velvet Santa pants.

I expect him to return his thumb to me now that I'm bare, but he pushes my hips down instead, dragging his eyes back to mine to watch my reaction as he grinds me against him. My eyes fight to stay open like air fights its way into my body with gasping breaths. The feel of the velvet against me without a barrier is like nothing I've ever felt. Soft and plush, but not smooth. I feel every fiber against my clit, every drag pulling me toward oblivion.

"I want you to make a mess of me, Rora. I want to feel your perfect cunt dripping all over me as you fall apart, getting good and ready for me to fuck you goddamn senseless after. You think you can do that for me, sugar?"

"I'll do anything for you," I say, surprising even myself. I'm more agreeable when I'm on the verge of a life-shattering orgasm. And based on the wicked smile that lights Henry's face, I guess he likes it.

"Good girl," he murmurs against my lips, moving me over his thigh in a circular motion that shatters me.

I cry his name, pressing my forehead against his as the orgasm ripples through me, cresting and falling in waves that feel like they last for hours. Henry doesn't stop, grinding me against him until my legs are shaking and my body is almost limp.

He wraps his arms around me in a bone-crushing hug. "You're so perfect," he says, pressing kisses all over my face. "Arms around my neck, baby."

I lift my arms with difficulty. He's already leeched the energy from me. How the hell am I supposed to survive him inside me?

"Hold on tight."

I don't have time to ask why before Henry stands, chuckling

at my squeak of surprise. I wrap my legs around his waist, and he carries me effortlessly, striding across the room. He pauses at the foot of the stairs and crouches down, grabbing a bag and slinging it over his shoulder with ease, like he's not carrying me at all, then takes the stairs two at a time.

Is this what it's like to be so tall? The ground feels too far away. How does he not get dizzy everywhere he goes?

"Which room?"

"Second on the left."

He nudges the door open with his knee and stops in the doorway. Peering over my shoulder, I clock the issue immediately. Ah.

I wince. "It's this or one of my parent's rooms."

"Twin bed it is," Henry replies, carrying me over to my childhood bed and laying me down.

I didn't think this part through. How the hell are we both going to squeeze on such a tiny bed?

I shuffle up the bed to make space for him, but he wraps a hand around my calf and tugs me back down. He drops to his knees between my thighs, spreads me open, and stops, just staring at me. His head is bowed slightly, so I can't see his expression.

"What are you doing?"

"Thinking."

"Thinking about what?" I ask, wariness creeping into my voice.

Henry looks up, his eyes crinkling. "All good things, sugar. I'm just deciding if I want to feel you coming on my mouth or fingers next."

Jesus. He drags his gaze over me like he's inspecting something with the utmost detail.

Thank you, past Rora, for spending extra time shaving.

"Do I get a say?" I ask, fighting the urge to squeeze my legs closed to his appraisal. I'm not usually self-conscious, but I've never been stared at so intently, either.

"Nope," Henry replies. "I'm going with both." He releases his hold on my thigh to tug my underwear off, but I still feel his handprints like they're burned into my skin.

My body collapses back against the bed as he draws one finger through my lips, circling my clit just once before pressing the tip inside me.

"Relax, baby," he murmurs.

Shit, I didn't even notice myself tensing. I suck in a deep breath, intent on breathing out the tension, but Henry pushes his finger further inside me, and the breath rushes out of me.

"Oh my fucking— *Fuck.*"

He pulls out and presses two fingers into me. God, if his fingers are this big… I have no time to worry about anything else because he curls his fingers and bends his head, running the flat of his tongue over my clit, and I think my brain switches off for a second.

His tongue moves slowly in long, languid strokes, but his fingers are another story. He's rough, alternating fucking me hard, massaging my G-spot, and scissoring his fingers, stretching me around him. I thrash, fisting the sheets as pressure builds in my core. He nips gently at my clit, and my back arches. I grab for his hair, but my fingers close around velvet.

The hat. I forgot about the fucking hat.

The velvet beneath my fingertips—the reminder of what we're doing, of how he's dressed—is my undoing. I splinter, my mouth falling open in a soundless scream. My chest burns as the orgasm courses through me, stealing the air from my lungs.

Henry changes it up, his fingers slowing and his tongue moving over me furiously like he's desperate to taste every drop of the orgasm he's given me.

Orgasms, I remind myself. He's made me come twice, and he's still fully dressed. Mostly, anyway.

When he pulls back, I take him in. Fuck, he's gorgeous. He's not just tall but broad, with a soft round belly and tattoos inked over every inch of his chest that I'm dying to trace with my tongue.

He's dressed exactly as he was during the shoot, like he was when we met—his jacket open, no shirt. His hat is barely hanging on, and his beard is glistening with... *Fuck*. With me.

I reach for him, and he stands, leaning over me. Once he's close enough, I wrap my still-shaking fingers around the white faux fur trim of his jacket and tug him in until he's close enough to kiss, close enough to feel his cock hard against me. Holy shit. I taste myself on his tongue the second his mouth is on mine, mingled with the sweet taste of Henry.

My fingers slip inside his jacket, tracing down the line of his suspenders. Henry smiles against my lips, drawing back.

"I assume it's not a coincidence that you're also dressed like you were when we met."

"I thought you might want the chance to look as much as you wanted to. Not that you were pretending not to look earlier."

"I'm a photographer. It's my job to thoroughly inspect every element of what I'm photographing."

He quirks a brow. "Every element, huh, sugar?"

I push him back, finding a new wave of energy despite two mind-blowing orgasms. I nudge his jacket off, taking my time slowly sliding the suspenders over his shoulders and tugging off his belt. Henry watches me, his breathing ragged.

I hook my thumbs in the waistband of both his pants and underwear. "Every element," I reply before pushing them down. Though my eyes want to wander, I watch his face.

He swallows, his throat bobbing.

I look down his body slowly, my eyes widening. "Oh my god."

I look from his cock to him and back again, opening and closing my mouth like a fish. Henry looks increasingly amused, just letting me take it all in. Visually. There's no way I'm taking it all in any other way. It's by far the biggest I've seen live and in person, thick and smooth. And massive. Absolutely fucking massive.

"I lied."

"About?"

"I'm not five-three. I'm five feet. Almost. I'm four-nine"

He laughs like I've surprised him, cupping my face without even bending because his arms are so long. "I know, sugar. I have eyes."

"Right. But what I mean is... This?" I point from his cock to me. "Not going to fit. Zero chance."

Henry shakes his head, a cocky, well-earned smile spreading over his face. "It's going to fit, baby." He steps out of his pants and underwear, nodding up the bed.

My body listens, even though my brain is telling me this is a terrible idea if I want to walk at any point over the next three to five business days.

I take deep, measured breaths while he roots around his bag and withdraws a strip of condoms, a small towel, and a bottle of lube, tossing them beside me on the bed. Thank fuck.

"I'm guessing you run into this a lot."

"I know to come prepared." Henry looks skeptically at the small mattress, but he kneels between my thighs and steadies himself by holding onto the headboard. His cock settles against my stomach, hard and heavy. "If we're going to do this, I'm going to make sure you're comfortable, but if you want to stop, we stop. There's zero pressure here, Rora."

I swear, the bar is on the goddamn floor. Why is that the nicest thing anyone's ever said to me during sex? Fuck it. I can take pictures sitting down if I have to.

"Okay." It sounds shakier than I'd like, my voice cracking on the second syllable. I clear my throat. "I want to. Fuck, I really want to." I swallow. "Will you put the jacket back on?" I'm cringing inside, but it's worth it as I watch Henry's eyes darken.

He nods, stepping off the bed and shrugging the jacket on. "Hat too?"

I can't stop the whimper that escapes me, which is answer enough, but I nod anyway.

Henry sets the hat on his head and drags his eyes all the way up my body before meeting mine. Amusement dances in his eyes when he kneels between my legs again, every bit the picture of my filthiest festive fantasy.

He presses our foreheads together, his lips hovering over mine. "You hate that you're into this, don't you?"

"Fucking Christmas," I mutter, and he grins.

"Sounds like something someone on the naughty list would say, sugar."

"I get the feeling you like me naughty, *Santa*."

"Fuck yeah, I do." Henry tears into a foil packet and rolls the condom over himself.

He runs the head of his cock over my clit, and my head falls back, a long, drawn-out curse escaping my lips. I watch through half-closed eyes as he opens the lube and drizzles some in his hand. He fists his cock, then wipes his hand on the towel.

"We're going to take it nice and slow," Henry promises, leaning in and pressing a soft kiss to my lips. "Tell me if you need a break."

"I can handle it," I reply as if I didn't say exactly the opposite five minutes ago.

Henry sits back on his knees and spreads my thighs, positioning himself against me. "I know you can."

He uses one thumb to trace gentle, rhythmic circles on my clit while he presses the head of his cock inside me. The sting as I stretch around him is immediate, but I draw in a long breath, pushing my head back into the pillows and focusing on the feel of his thumb on the clit.

"Rora—"

"I'm okay. Don't stop. Please." I'm so fucking close to

begging him to just fuck me. He's so polite, the perfect gentleman. Well, as much of a gentleman as he can be, considering he has me naked and desperate beneath him.

A feral groan escapes Henry's lips as he bottoms out inside of me. My childhood bedroom falls away, my senses focusing on him and only him. The hazy look of bliss on his face through my half-closed eyes, the gleam of sweat forming on his brow. The sweet peppermint scent flooding my veins.

Our mingled gasping breaths, whimpers, and half-formed curses as he moves inside me.

The feel of him, heavy and steady on top of me, pleasure coiling like a viper ready to strike wherever he touches me.

And the taste of him, the taste of *us*, on his tongue when he leans in to steal my mouth.

He's more than I could ever capture on film. But that doesn't stop me from wishing I could. I could so easily get hooked on this.

Oh god, I can't get hooked on this.

But that doesn't stop me from wishing I could.

Henry threads his fingers through mine, caging my head with our hands, pressing them into the pillows.

"Fuck, baby. You feel goddamn incredible."

I try to reply that no, *he* feels goddamn incredible, but all that comes out is a garbled cry as Henry fucks me deeper, harder. He squeezes my hands tight, his thrusts jolting my entire body. I can hardly feel my legs anymore, clinging to his waist for dear life. I'm entirely at his mercy, his to fuck and use as he pleases, and Henry knows it.

"You like being in control?" I ask, each word accented with a gasp.

Henry runs his nose along my jaw, breathing me in. "I like you trusting me enough to let me." A shiver ricochets down my spine as he nips my earlobe with his teeth. "I like feeling how much you like it." His lips traverse my throat, the gentle kisses he places in the crook of my neck at odds with the rough strokes of his cock inside me. "I like knowing that, just for right now, you're all mine. That every groan from your perfect lips, every squeeze of your beautiful cunt, is just for me. Actually, I don't like that," he says, his lips somehow back on mine. "I fucking love it."

I'm treading the precipice of something reckless, lightning snapping at my heels, ready to toss me over the edge and drag me down into the depths of somewhere no one has ever taken me. I already know Henry's filthy mouth will have a starring role in my mind long after we both leave Wintermore, but in these moments, it feels like nothing is ever going to feel so good again. I want to draw it out, make each second last an hour, but he makes it impossible.

"I can feel how close you are." His voice is low and husky, his Southern drawl thicker like he usually holds it back but isn't in control of himself right now. "Let me have it. Fall apart for me, sugar."

How the fuck can I say no to that?

My body gives me no choice, soaring over the cliff's edge and plummeting deep, deep, deeper into Henry. I squeeze his hands so hard I know my nails will leave imprints, my back bowing what little it can under Henry's weight.

He curses, blowing out a long breath that tickles my cheek, and I open my eyes just in time to see every muscle in his face going slack.

"Rora," he whispers as he comes, complete and utter ecstasy overtaking his features.

I can't get hooked on this. I can't get hooked on him. But that doesn't stop me from wishing I could.

7
HENRY
December 7

I've never been a lazy morning person. When I was younger, there was always so much to do, so much to learn, so much ravenous excitement for the world around me. I got into the habit of waking up and jumping straight out of bed, ready to take on the day. And there's no reason to stay in bed at the research station—they're uncomfortable as all hell.

But there's something about Rora that makes me want to drag out this morning for as long as possible. She's still fast asleep, half on top of me, her blonde hair strewn across my chest. The shorter pieces that usually frame her face flutter as she breathes deeply, her face softer in sleep.

God, she really was onto something with the whole "he sees you when you're sleeping" thing. It's intimate—not something I'd usually let myself enjoy—but I don't want it to end.

Soft pink light streaks through Rora's tangerine curtains, beaming a hazy orange glow across the room. It's not what I'd have expected from her room. Glow-in-the-dark stars are dotted across the ceiling, the kind I remember being all the rage in the 90s. Sunrise colors cover every inch of the room: yellow, pink, orange, and purple. It's a perfect balance of soft, bright, and summery, the antithesis of the town that celebrates Christmas year-round.

I raise a hand, running a finger over the wing of one of the fabric butterflies pinned in a line going up the wall like they're flying.

"Those were a Pottery Barn special back in 2010. Everyone wanted them—well, all pre-teen girls did, anyway," Rora finishes with a yawn, stretching out so the blankets slip down to her waist. "Morning."

"Mornin'." I swallow, trying not to be a creep who can't stop staring at her. But she's so fucking beautiful—even more so in the morning, lit by the glow of the sunrise, her eyes still heavy with sleep. "When did you last change anything in here?"

"My sophomore year of high school, maybe? I didn't spend much time here after my parents both started traveling again. I mostly stayed with—" She cuts herself off as if she doesn't want to mention my family, like doing so will burst the little bubble we've sequestered ourselves away in.

But The Enchanted Workshop opens in a few hours, and we have to show up and act like we didn't spend the night together. Just the thought has me tightening my hold on her.

The bubble is already at breaking point. If we don't want things to be weird, we're just going to have to pretend they're not already weird. Which means talking about my family just like we did before last night.

"It's good that you had them," I say before I lose my nerve.

A slightly raised brow is the only sign Rora's surprised I'm talking about them.

"I was lucky to. Still am. I talk to them all the time when I travel. And when I come back... It's like I never left." She doesn't need to spell it out for me to know that Rora considers them family, just like I know my brother considers her one of his own.

Which makes this all the weirder. I can't imagine Charlie would be remotely okay with Rora and me hooking up, but at least I don't have to worry about coming between her and Noelle.

"I ran into Noelle on the way here," I tell her. "She said you asked her if she was okay with this."

Rora searches my face like she's trying to see if I'm upset by her talking to Noelle. "It seemed like the right thing to do. Are you… Is it okay that I did?"

I run my hand down her back, tracing her spine. "I'm glad you did. It made me realize you'd actually been thinking about this and it wasn't a spur-of-the-moment thing because we'd been flirting earlier."

"Oh, I've been thinking about it. Constantly."

"Would it be weird if I said I had, too?"

Her brows knit together. "Why would it be weird?"

"Y-you know," I stammer, gesturing at nothing and every-thing. "You're so… I'm a lot older than you. I don't want you to think I've been sexualizing you or anything."

Amusement flashes in her eyes. "Henry, you were inside me less than twelve hours ago. I think it's safe to say I'm okay with you sexualizing me."

Blood rushes to my cheeks. "I guess that's true. But I'm out of my depth here. I don't normally do this."

"Casual sex?"

"Casual sex, I do. Just not usually with people almost twenty years younger than me. And then there's the whole complicated family element…"

Rora wrinkles her nose and lifts her shoulder in a shrug. "I'll admit the family element is a little weird, but I'm an adult."

Shit. This is coming out wrong. "I know you are. But you're an adult who's the same age as my niece. It'd be worrying if I wasn't at least a little hesitant."

"I'll give you that," Rora replies with a snort. "For the record, this isn't something I do either."

"So, the Santa kink isn't a year-round thing?" I tease, and Rora scowls.

"It's not a— Shut up. I meant the casual sex with people

almost twenty years older than me," she mimics me, rolling her eyes. "Or casual sex at all."

"Seriously? But you're always traveling. Do you do long distance?"

Rora tugs the covers back up over her shoulders and snuggles into me. "Nope. Honestly, I'm not usually interested in people like this. Occasionally, I meet someone I'm attracted to and want to hook up with"—she gestures to me—"but it doesn't happen often. It's been a while, actually."

Curiosity gets the better of me. "How long is a while?"

"Ten months, maybe? Yeah, it must be," she confirms after thinking it over. "The last person I hooked up with was a woman in Boston last Halloween who was *really* into biting. Took me a couple of months to heal."

"Damn. That makes the Santa kink look pretty tame, sugar."

She grabs a pillow that's an inch from falling off the bed and whacks me with it.

"What about you? Do you do the long-distance thing? I'm guessing opportunities to meet people are thin on the ground in Greenland."

"I try not to get involved with anyone I work with regularly, but we get a lot of guest researchers at our station. Long distance is a no for me. I've done it twice and never again."

"That bad?"

"Awful. The first time wasn't the worst. We just fought all the time, and we were miserable for two years before she ended things. The second time, he just stopped calling one day, and a few months later, I found out he had a husband and kids."

Rora grimaces. "Ouch."

"Right? I'm too clingy for long-distance, anyway."

"Oh, I can totally see you being clingy," she says, laughing at my answering frown.

I lightly pinch her waist, and she squeaks, trying to wriggle

away from me but just ending up breathless and practically straddling me.

We still, my breath catching in my throat. The blankets are
well and truly gone, bunched up at the foot of the bed, leaving us
both naked.

Rora inhales, tracing the swirl of the cloud tattoo covering my
left pec, then resting her hand flat on my chest. I can't tell if her
hand is cold or my skin is just blazing, but a shiver snakes
through me.

"I like these. Are they all related to the Arctic?"

"Mostly."

She listens with rapt attention as I talk her through my tattoos:
the clouds, iceberg, the top-down view of the arctic circle on my
chest, and the arctic animals winding around my right arm. My
left arm is covered in mountains and trees, and...

"A single Christmas tree," I point out. It's not obvious if
you're not looking for it.

I expect her to give me shit for it, but her eyes soften. "This is
the same one Charlie has."

"We got them before I moved to Washington for my PhD and
promised we'd always spend Christmas together. I think we knew
it wouldn't be possible forever, but it was a nice thought." Charlie's seven years older than me and was already married with two
kids by the time I left Texas.

"They're all beautiful," Rora says, nodding at my tattoos, "but
the Christmas tree is my favorite." She glances at the clock on the
nightstand and frowns. "I suppose we should get ready for work."

"Probably, yeah."

But Rora doesn't move right away. She looks at my tattoos,
then the window, then her lap—everywhere but my face. I know
where this is going before she even opens her mouth. It's the only
way this *can* go, but I was more okay with that yesterday than I
am this morning.

"I'm glad we did this," she says, sitting back and pulling her hands away from my chest.

"Me too."

"But you're right: it's complicated and a little weird. I like you, but we're both leaving, and we're going to run into each other over the years at family things."

"Yeah. We should probably just cut this off at one night and enjoy it for what it was."

Rora nods, but her eyes are as dull as I feel. "Exactly." She swings her leg over me and gracefully hops down. "But there is one thing I want you to do."

"What?"

She grabs my phone from the nightstand and hands it to me. "Call your boss and accept the job. Last night proves that stepping out of your comfort zone can be fun."

I close my fist around the phone, smiling. "You might be right. I'll call."

"Good." Rora crouches down and picks up my pants from where I dropped them. "We should've thrown these in the wash last night. I don't suppose they can go in the dryer?"

I chuckle, remembering how worried she was about messing them up last night. "They're dry clean only, but I have a spare pair."

"Of course you do." She narrows her eyes at them. "Were you wearing the suit when you ran into Noelle last night?"

I wince and nod.

"Oh god," she groans, closing her eyes. "I'm never going to live this down."

8
RORA

December 10

"Now, remember to be extra good, and we'll see what we can do about getting you that racing track, Austin."

"Thank you, Santa!"

I look up from behind my laptop as Henry helps the kid down from the throne, giving him one last hug and handing him one of the stockings we give to all the kids who visit Santa. The little boy hugs it tight to his chest.

Henry really is in his element with the kids. It's hard to imagine him on a research station in remote Greenland with just a handful of other scientists and visitors. It's harder not to let the sight of it turn me into a puddle.

His new job, which he officially accepted before work on Wednesday morning, sounds more like him: traveling the world and meeting new people every few weeks.

I hit send on the pictures, uploading them to the tablet by the cash register, where people can scroll through the pictures, add pre-set filters, and pick their favorites to have printed.

"Noelle will take you through the pictures at the register," I tell Austin's grandma, my old high school guidance counselor.

"Thank you, Rora. God, I can't believe how grown up you are." Ms. Herrera shakes her head like she's offended by the mere thought of time. "Austin, honey, say thank you to Rora."

"Thank you, Miss Rora!" Austin throws his little arms around my legs and squeezes me.

"You're welcome, kiddo. Have a great Christmas," I tell them.

"I know better than to say the same to you," Ms. Herrera replies with a laugh, waving as she and her grandson leave the grotto.

"Your reputation precedes you," Henry says from his throne.

When I look up, he's smiling softly, and I have to look away. Because if I look at him in full Santa attire for so long without the shield of my camera, I'll forget everything I said about things being complicated and climb on his lap in the middle of the toy store. The past few days have been fucking torture.

"My hatred of Christmas is well known in this town. There's been more than one intervention over the years." Said interventions usually involved Christmas cookies, at least. "You ready for the next kid?"

"Let's do it."

I cross the grotto and pull open the curtain, only for a small curly-haired girl dressed head to toe in pink to run inside before I can call, *Next!* I share a look of surprise with Henry before taking her in. She's older than most kids who come to see Santa and oddly familiar. Which probably means her family is local.

"Hi," she says, looking up at me expectantly. Oh, to have the confidence of children.

"Hi. I'm Rora. What's your name?"

"Ava."

"Nice to meet you, Ava. Do you have a grownup with you?"

"My dad," she replies. "But he lets me do things on my own. I'm almost nine."

"That's pretty grown up, but we need your dad here too," I explain as an all too familiar voice calls her name behind the curtain.

"In here, Dad!"

Sophie Snow

I brace myself as the curtain opens, bringing me face to face with my senior-year boyfriend.

Kenny's eyes widen, his jaw dropping. "Holy shit! It's Sour Stanley!"

Nine and a half years. It's been almost a decade since I left, and I still haven't escaped the fucking nickname.

"Hey, Kenny."

He rushes forward and pulls me into a hug that I begrudgingly return.

I haven't seen Kenny since graduation, but we broke up amicably. He was someone I liked enough to have fun with before escaping Wintermore, but it was never going to be anything more.

I look up over Kenny's shoulder to see Henry glaring at his back. He notices my gaze and quickly changes his expression into something more neutral.

"Why did you call her that, Dad?" Ava interrupts, giving me a chance to pull out of Kenny's grip.

His eyes widen as he realizes he has to explain the shitty nickname to his kid. "Oh, um…" He looks at me for help, but he's not getting anything out of me. "Well, Rora was younger… She liked sour candy and didn't smile a lot, so people started calling her Sour Stanley in middle school." God forbid a woman doesn't smile.

I sneak a look at Henry, who's back to glaring at Kenny.

Ava turns to me, crossing her arms. "Why don't you smile? Are you sad?"

Jesus Christ. "I'm not sad. I'm just not a smiley person."

"That's cool," Ava replies. "My nana says you don't have to smile just because someone tells you to."

"That's good advice. Do you want to meet Santa?" Ava seems sweet, but the faster I can get her out of here, the less likely Kenny is to start reminiscing.

The second the question crosses my lips, Ava's entire demeanor changes. She shrinks, shadows crossing her face.

"Come on. You wanted to do this," Kenny complains.

I ignore him, crouching down so I'm at eye level with Ava. "What are you thinking?"

She bites her lip. "Some boys at school said Santa's not real and I'm too old to sit in his lap for pictures."

I wasn't raised to believe in Santa, but my parents made damn sure I knew other kids believed and it wasn't okay to tell them otherwise. I still remember how devastated Noelle was when she found out.

"Well, that's just silly of them, isn't it?" I tell Ava. "Of course Santa's real. He's right there." I point to Henry, and Ava peeks shyly over her shoulder.

Henry gives her a little wave, smiling widely. "Hi, Ava."

She gasps, turning back to me, her eyes sparkling. "He knows my name!" she whisper-screams.

"Santa knows everyone's names. He's magic," I tell her, and her eyes go wide with excitement. "And you don't have to sit in his lap to get your picture taken."

"I don't?"

"Nope. In fact…" I reach behind my little desk setup and pull out a fluffy bear in an elf costume. "This is Snowball, and she's Mrs. Claus's favorite bear. Mrs. Claus really wants some pictures of Snowball and Santa together, but Snowball doesn't like sitting on Santa's lap either. Maybe you could stand beside Santa and hold her so I can take some pictures for Mrs. Claus?"

She practically tears the bear out of my hand, skipping excitedly over to stand beside Henry.

Kenny whistles. "Shit, you're good at this."

"I've been doing it a long time." I love taking pictures of kids. They usually don't have the same hang-ups about the camera that adults do, and I love seeing their personalities shine through in pictures. They just need to feel heard.

We're only three hours into the day, but my neck is killing me. I need to get a more comfortable camera strap. Rolling my neck, I pull my camera over my head. I don't often take pictures without it, but it's not like my camera is at risk in the grotto.

Ava is a lot less shy with the bear in her arms, giving a toothy grin to the camera.

"I think we got it," I call, giving Ava a thumbs-up after flicking through the previews. I transfer the images to my laptop and set my camera on the table while Henry does the usual "what do you want for Christmas" routine. Usually, grownups hover near the throne to listen, but Kenny barely spares a glance for his daughter. I make a mental note to check with Henry what Ava wants for Christmas so I can pass it on later.

Kenny leans over the desk, propping his face up on his elbows. "How long are you in town for?"

I sort through the pictures on my laptop, not looking up. "Not sure yet."

"We should hook up while you're here. Go out for a drink or something."

Noelle and I are going to be having a talk after work. She checks everyone in for Santa pictures; a little warning that Kenny was in line would've been nice.

"I don't think so, but thanks."

"Come on, Ror. It'll be just like old times," Kenny whines, and I fight the urge to roll my eyes. Apparently, becoming a dad hasn't matured him any. "I'm not with Ava's mom, if that's what you're worried about."

"Nope. I just don't want to."

A shadow looms over Kenny's back, and I look up to see Henry walking over with Ava in tow. He rarely leaves the throne while families are in here, but he also doesn't usually glare daggers at them.

"You did great, Ava." I hold out my fist, and she bumps it before handing the bear over. "Mrs. Claus is going to love these pictures."

"Thank you for letting me hold Snowball. I can't wait to tell everyone at school!"

Beside her, Kenny rolls his eyes. "Don't do that. You're just going to get upset when they—"

"Actually, Ava," Henry interrupts Kenny, smiling down at her. "We try not to tell too many people about Snowball, so she stays nice and safe. We wouldn't want everyone rushing in here and asking to take pictures with her."

Ava mimics locking her lips. "I'll keep your secret." She flings her arms around my waist.

I like *these* kinds of hugs. But when Ava lets go, her dad surges forward, spreading his arms wide and saying, "My turn."

I watch in horror as his arm connects with my camera, launching it from the desk. Time stands still for a moment as both Henry and I lunge for it, but not long enough for either of us to stop it connecting with the hardwood with a sickening crunch.

9
HENRY
December 10

N oelle is ranting about Rora's ex when I finish changing and meet them in the back room. Rora has changed out of her costume and she's sitting at the table, her head propped on her hands, staring at the wreck of her camera like she can fix it with sheer willpower. If anyone could, I suspect it would be her.

I slide past Noelle and drop into the seat beside her. "Is it fixable?"

She pulls it toward us, running a finger over the large crack running down the mirror on the front. The casing is busted, mangled insides peeking out. Even with next to no knowledge of camera, I know the lens is a lost cause. It's completely shattered.

"In theory, it's fixable," Rora says with a sigh. "It would be a long shot, but it would also cost a hell of a lot more to repair it than replace it."

"Surely your insurance will replace it," Noelle says, taking a seat opposite us.

Rora closes her eyes and rubs her forehead, a pained expression crossing her face. "They would…"

"Oh my god. Rora, tell us you have insurance."

Rora groans, throwing her hands up at Noelle's question. "Insurance was a perk of my job, and I didn't think I'd need it here. I've looked into it, but I wasn't planning on getting it until I leave."

She sounds so fucking done with everything, and it's instinctive to reach out and rub a hand over her back. It's the first time I've touched her since we climbed out of bed, and Rora tenses for a moment before her whole body seems to relax into my touch. I avoid looking at Noelle, not wanting to see her reaction to me comforting her best friend like this.

"You should make Kenny pay for the replacement," Noelle growls and Rora laughs, but there's not a shred of humor in her voice.

"As much as I'd love to, I can't imagine he has several thousand dollars sitting aside for this. I have savings; I can manage it. It's just... Shit. Not what I needed right now." She shakes her head, grabbing her purse from the floor and rummaging through it. "It's a popular model, so I shouldn't have any problems replacing it, at least. I'll head up to Jackson now, so we can open the grotto again tomorrow morning."

"Are you sure? That's a lot of driving in the snow," Noelle protests.

"It's a three-hour round trip. That's nothing." Rora pulls a set of keys from her purse.

Before I know what I'm doing, I reach across and snag them from her fingers. "I'll drive."

Rora blinks in surprise. Noelle leans back in her seat, her arms crossed.

"Oh, you don't have to. It's a lot of driving."

"As you literally just pointed out, it's a three-hour round trip. That's nothing," I repeat. She frowns at me, but it doesn't reach her eyes. "You've had a stressful day. Let me do this for you, sugar."

Rora's lips remain down-turned, but her eyes soften. "I hate how easily that fucking accent works on me."

"Sure you do." I stand up and squeeze her shoulder. "Give me five minutes to get your car warmed up before you come out. I don't want you to be cold."

Noelle's voice follows me down the hall. "This is interesting."
Followed by Rora's unmistakable groan and, "Shut up."

10
RORA
December 10

As shit as today has been, I'm not so cut up about it that I can't appreciate the sight of Henry, one hand on the steering wheel, flying down the snowy highway like a pro. He made good on his promise of warming up the car, so much so that I pulled off my sweater, scarf, and gloves five minutes after we pulled out of the parking lot.

I unwrap a lemon candy and set it on my tongue, breathing a sigh of relief as the sour taste hits me and Wintermore disappears in the rearview, replaced by the powder sugar dusted mountains lining the highway.

What a fucking day. *What a fucking year*, I mentally correct myself.

Wyoming is beautiful when I'm not being subjected to inflatable snowmen and Christmas music being blasted into the streets. Noelle has never been a fan of the mountains looming over the town. She says they make her feel small and insignificant, but I love them.

My parents moved to Wyoming for the mountains, and I took my first steps on a winter morning when I spotted a moose peeking out of the forest beside our campsite. My mom snapped a picture of me reaching for it, then handed me off to my dad and disappeared for half an hour, returning with a camera full of pictures of the moose meandering through the trees. One of those pictures ended up on the cover of an international wildlife magazine, but, to this day, my mom swears the picture she took of me is the best she's ever taken. She keeps a crinkled copy in her wallet and shows it off to everyone she meets, telling them how proud she is of me.

I turn away from the Mountain View, staring straight ahead down the highway instead.

"You alright?"

"Mm-hmm."

Henry drums his fingers on the steering wheel. "You want to try that again, sugar?"

Sugar. The drawl. For fuck's sake.

I glare at him. "Stop calling me 'sugar' like that because you know it makes me more agreeable."

Henry's lips lift in a sinful smirk. "I don't think I will, actually." He sets his free hand on my knee, and my heart pauses. I can still feel the ghost of his touch from a few days ago. "I'm sorry today's been so rough."

Should I be concerned that he can make my breath catch with just a hand on my leggings?

"Thank you. And thank you for driving me."

"Anytime," Henry says with a smile, his blue eyes twinkling, even though we both know it's not true.

In a few weeks, we'll both be on our way out of Wyoming, and who the hell knows when we're going to cross paths again? That thought has me reaching out to brush the edge of Henry's hand with my pinky. Electricity sizzles where my skin touches his, and I pull my hand back. I look away, staring out the window but seeing nothing. I feel the heat of Henry's gaze roaming over me before returning to the road, but he doesn't remove his hand.

Silence stretches between us like elastic pulled to the breaking point as we continue down the highway. The occasional car passes us in the other direction, but the road is quiet.

"You're awful tense over there." Henry's hold on my knee is loose, casual, but he grips the steering while like a vise.

"It's been a stressful day." Not a lie, but not the truth behind the fraught tension between us.

Henry hums, a noncommittal sound of agreement low in his throat. His fingers twitch on my knee. "I reckon I could help you out with that."

His words suck all the air from the car, muffling the sound of the tires skating over the salt on the road. I look up, but his eyes are trained ahead. My hand itches to reach for his.

It feels inevitable; why bother to resist? Did we really think we could spend the rest of the season stuck in a ten-by-ten room, content with the memories of one night? A perfect night, sure, but I've never been satisfied with perfect. I always crave just a little more, like I have to keep proving perfection wrong.

"We shouldn't. It was supposed to be just one night." It's barely a protest, but I tell myself it's enough to say it, even if I don't mean it. My voice is barely a whisper, so hushed I'm not sure he hears me until he replies.

"I've never been good at doing what I'm supposed to. And something tells me you're not either."

"I'm not." I let myself reach for his hand, gasping at the electric shock where our skin meets.

Henry's shoulders relax, the tension between us snapping as he turns his head and meets my eyes. He brings my hand to his lips, pressing a kiss to my palm in the split second his eyes are off the road. "Take off your leggings."

His words don't register right away, and even when they do, I'm not sure I've heard him right. "Take my leggings off … here? We're on the highway; people could see."

"And here I thought you liked being watched, baby."

When it's just me and Henry in the privacy of my living room, sure. But flying down the highway just shy of sixty miles per hour where anyone could see us…

Why the fuck is that turning me on?

It's Henry; it has to be. There's no other explanation for me suddenly developing not only a Santa kink but, apparently, a touch of exhibitionism.

"Fuck." It falls from my lips like a resigned whisper.

Henry's low chuckle sounds in the car as I inhale a deep breath of cool mountain air. I know better than to undo my seat-belt on a snowy highway, even for a second. I lift myself as much as it allows and wriggle my leggings over my ass, and I have to kick my boots off to remove them entirely; the whole thing is completely ungraceful, but Henry's eyes are on the road.

I sit back down in the seat, my heart racing. I'm sitting in nothing but my underwear and a shirt in a car that technically belongs to my mom. *What the fuck am I doing?*

Every anxious thought disappears in a flash when Henry's warm fingers land on my bare skin. "Breathe. This is supposed to be calming."

"I'm calm."

Henry tuts, his fingers creeping up my thigh and pausing over my underwear. The thin cotton is no match for the heat of his fingers. My eyes flutter closed, my legs trembling with the urge to do the same.

"Lying is a naughty list offense, sugar." He slides his hand inside my underwear and sucks in a gasp. "But *fuck*, you feel so damn nice. You're so wet, baby. Is this all for me?"

"Fuck, Henry," I whimper. "Yes. *Yes*."

He presses one finger down on my clit, and my legs snap closed, trapping his hand. I'm semi-consciously aware that this makes Henry driving with one hand on the wheel even *less* safe, but it's hard to care when he's circling my clit like he's striking flint against steel, and I'm seconds from going up in flames.

I protest when he stops, but Henry lifts my leg over his thigh, spreading me open. "Keep this here for me." He runs his hand up my calf, my thigh, sliding it back in my underwear.

The road is getting busier the closer to Jackson we get, and I make eye contact with the driver of a passing Jeep at the exact second Henry presses a finger inside me. I throw my head back against the headrest, my back arching against the seat. His hands are so fucking big that he has his middle finger inside me, doing incredible things to my G-spot, while his thumb swipes back and forth over my clit.

I clench around his finger, sobbing his name. "I'm so... Fuck, I'm so close."

Henry's voice is gravelly when he responds. "Lift your shirt, sugar."

I do as I'm told, the other cars on the road barely crossing my mind. I'm wearing my favorite bra: black, strapless, and plunging. Henry steals a quick glance at me, groaning as I palm my breasts, squeezing them.

"God, Rora." For the first time, his fingers falter, and I realize this is affecting him almost as much as it is me.

I move my leg, trying to shift my foot closer to Henry's cock.

"I wouldn't do that unless you want me to crash this car," he warns. It still takes me a second to pull my leg back, begrudgingly. "Good girl," Henry says with a pained chuckle, rewarding me by pressing a second finger inside me. "You're driving me wild, sugar."

Flames lash me, spreading over my skin like wildfire. "Shit. I... Fuck, Henry, I can't. I—"

"You can. Show everyone how pretty you are when you come for me, sugar."

Everyone. The reminder that any passerby could look in the car and see what we're doing knocks me off my axis. The road blurs before my eyes, fireworks exploding inside me.

Henry coaxes me through it with hushed, barely discernible praise and slow circles over my clit. By the time I'm coming back into myself, the tinny voice of the GPS is directing him to pull into the strip mall carpark. He heads for the empty far corner. Whoever plowed the parking lot didn't even bother coming in this far, making it the perfect hidden spot for me to undo my seatbelt and swing onto Henry's lap the second he puts the car in park.

Am I proud of the way I practically shove my tongue down his throat? No. But the sweet taste of him mixed with the lingering lemon on my tongue is incredible.

His cock is pressing hard against his jeans, and I grind down on him, knotting my hands in his hair. Henry groans into my mouth, slipping his hands inside my underwear and squeezing my ass. He bites down on my lip, and I roll my hips over him.

Henry gasps, pressing his forehead to mine. "Fuck. *Fuck*." He comes with a shudder, gripping my ass hard enough to leave marks.

I hope he leaves marks.

He draws his hands up my back, wrapping them around me in a bear hug, panting. "I don't think I've come in my pants since high school."

"That's so hot." The words slip out without thought, but I'm too blissed out to care that I sound like an early 2000s reality TV star. Or to think too hard about the mess Henry's going to be dealing with until we make it back to Wintermore.

Henry leans his head back against the headrest, a lazy smile on his face. "I fucking love your car."

"It's actually my mom's car."

His smile falls away, and I can't help but laugh at the look of horror that replaces it. "I wish I could go back in time ten seconds before I knew that."

11
HENRY

December 10

Rora's cheeks are rosy, but we can blame that on the cold. My underwear took the brunt of our parking lot fun. Thank god I wore black jeans to work this morning. I cleaned up as best as I could in the driver's seat, but I don't care how messy things got; feeling Rora come on my fingers, watching her so desperate for me that she climbed onto my lap the second I stopped the car, is the hottest thing that's ever happened to me. *Rora* is the hottest thing that's ever happened to me.

A soft bell chimes above the door as we enter the camera store, stomping the snow from our boots on the welcome mat. A woman looks up from behind the counter, her face lighting up behind thick, purple-framed glasses.

"Is that my Rora girl?" She drops the magazine in her hand and rushes out from behind the counter, scooping Rora up in her arms.

"Hey, Bobbi." Rora hugs her before introducing us. "Bobbi's been friends with my parents for years," she explains as Bobbi leads us across the store.

She leans against the counter, pushing her glasses up her nose. "I can't believe you're here at this time of year. I haven't seen snow in your hair since you were a teenager."

"I had a … break from work, and Noelle's usual Santa photographer bailed, so she asked me to come home," Rora says, brushing the snow from her hair. It lands on her shoulders, melting into her sweater.

"And I bet you're hating every second of it."

Rora glances my way for a second before replying, "Not every second."

The urge to reach for her, to wrap my arms around her and press my lips to the top of her head, is intense. And not exactly in line with just one night at her place and an orgasm in the car. *Fuck.*

If Bobbi notices the threads of tension between us, she doesn't comment. "I know you didn't drive all the way up here in the snow just to see me. What's going on, my girl?"

Rora reaches into her tote bag and pulls out the wreckage, eliciting a gasp from Bobbi. A piece of the casing falls off as Rora sets the camera down on the counter and she winces.

"I suspect I already know, but do you think this can be fixed?"

"Can a bobcat outrun a pronghorn?"

Rora's brows meet in the middle. "No?"

"Then I'd say you're shit out of luck."

"That's what I figured." Rora sighs, rubbing her face with her hands. "Please tell me you have one in stock."

Bobbi picks up the camera and promptly puts it down when more of the casing crumbles in her hand. "This, we have. But the lens... I don't think we have this exact one. Antonio!" she hollers, drawing a lanky college-aged boy from the back.

I tune them out as they discuss lenses, brands, and all kinds of things that make zero sense to me. But it's nice to see Rora in her element. I love watching her take pictures, but we've barely left The Enchanted Workshop since we both arrived in town. This is the first time I've really seen her talking about the thing she loves most in the world with people who know what she's talking about. As stressed as she is about dropping her savings on a new camera, I can see the excitement in her eyes as she picks up different lenses to inspect them.

I want to know what else makes her light up like this. We've spent enough time together—breaks in the grotto between kids and decompressing in the back room on our lunch break—that I've noticed the little things she does. Like scrolling through Instagram and screenshotting things to send her parents because they, apparently, never check their Instagram messages. Or the way she takes a handheld gaming console everywhere with her. I don't know what she's playing, but I see how her shoulders relax whenever she's playing it. And then there's the sour candy. How many times have I seen her unwrap one of those little candies and breathe a happy little sigh when it hits her tongue?

I startle as Rora grasps my arm. "You okay? You kind of zoned out for a second there."

"Yeah, shit, sorry. Is that the one you're getting?" I ask, nodding to the camera and lens in her hand.

"I think so, but I'm going to run outside and see what I think of the lens in natural light. Want to come?"

"I'm going to look around, but take your time, sugar."

Rora squeezes my arm before letting go and heading outside with Antonio.

The second the door closes behind them, I pull my wallet from my pocket and turn to Bobbi. "Can you charge all of this to my card before she comes back in and gets pissed off at me?"

I hold out my card, and Bobbi plucks it from my fingers, chuckling. "You know her well."

Not as well as I'd like to.

She runs her eyes over my credit card and raises a brow. "Whitten. You're related to Noelle?"

I scratch the back of my neck. "She's my niece."

Something tells me Bobbi has never hidden a single emotion in her life. Shock crosses her face, morphing to mild distaste. It's a reasonable reaction to finding out the man hanging around the twenty-something you've known since she was a kid is not only much older than her but her best friend's uncle. It doesn't feel as weird as it did—she's an adult and perfectly capable of deciding who and what she wants—but I'm not naïve. I know how this looks.

I suppose it's a good thing that it was only one night at her place and one orgasm in the car. Even if just thinking that sours my stomach.

Bobbi swipes my card and turns the screen toward me, holding it just a little out of my reach. The number on the screen is staggering, but I've been living rent-free on a research station for over a decade and my new job has a significant salary increase. I'm lucky enough that I won't even notice a dent in my savings, and I don't want Rora depleting hers when she's still figuring shit out with her job.

"You're not paying for this because you expect something in return, are you?"

"Of course not," I answer immediately.

Bobbi looks unconvinced, and though I'm glad Rora has people on her side, I don't want to mention her job loss. I'm guessing she hasn't told her parents yet since they're off grid, and the last thing she needs right now is someone telling them before she can.

"Look, she's been having a rough couple of months, and she's stuck here at Christmas. I just don't want her to have to worry about money on top of that," I explain.

Bobbi pushes the screen toward me. "You seem like an okay guy, I suppose. And even if you *were* expecting something from her, Rora doesn't do anything she doesn't want to. That girl learned how to be headstrong from her parents and was more stubborn than them both by the time she started school. That's why we love her."

I sign the screen and turn away, peering out the window while Bobbi processes the payment. Rora's hair is fluttering in the breeze as she peers intently at the camera's preview screen, her face intense with concentration.

"She's something else," I agree with Bobbi, my lips pulling up in a grin when Rora looks up and catches me watching her.

She gives me a knowing look through the window before reentering the store and raising an eyebrow. "You're making a habit of this whole watching thing," she quips.

"I've been meaning to get a new hobby, and I've got to say, I'm really enjoying it."

Rora snorts, rolling her eyes as she sets the camera down on the counter.

"How's the lens?" From the outside, it looks exactly the same as her old one to me, but I'm sure Rora is going to make magic with it.

"It's good—versatile, which is what I look for. I hate carrying a bunch of stuff around with me," she grumbles, digging in her tote bag. She pulls her wallet and grimaces. "Just swipe my card and don't tell me the damage," she says, handing her card over.

Bobbi doesn't take it. "Actually…" *Shit. Here we go.* "It's already paid for."

Rora's face morphs from dread to confusion. "What do you…"

Bobbi's eyes flick quickly to me and back again, but Rora clocks it. She turns.

I try not to make eye contact with her, but *fuck*, her eyes are pretty. "Sugar, I—"

"No," she interrupts. "Absolutely fucking not. Refund him, please," she tells Bobbi.

"We don't actually do refunds," Antonio interjects, and Rora sucks in a breath.

"Then make an exception, Antonio." She sounds deadly calm, and Antonio looks like he's one second from bolting.

"We'll give you two a minute," Bobbi says, tugging Antonio into the back. Wise.

Rora whirls on me, but I grab her hand and she pauses before, presumably, tearing into me.

"Hear me out."

"There's nothing you can say that will make me okay with you spending thousands of dollars on me, Henry."

"I wanted to."

Rora blinks like she was expecting something more. Understandable, because that's a weak fucking excuse. "You … wanted to?"

"Yeah. I know you can afford it, but you shouldn't have to drain your savings because your asshole ex was trying to get handsy with you. And I like watching you take pictures, sugar."

She sighs but doesn't drop my hand. I take that as a good sign and step a little closer to her.

"I don't know what to say to that. *Thank you*, I guess, since I can tell I'm not going to change your mind."

"You're welcome."

Rora drops my hand, just to wrap her arms around my middle, resting her head against my chest. "You're a really good guy." She sounds resigned.

I hug her back, nestling one hand in her hair. "You seem real pissed off about that."

"You're making it difficult for me to do the things I should and not the things I want to. It's a problem for me."

And it's a problem for *me* how much I like hearing that.

12
RORA

December 10

I did the math on the ride to the restaurant: seven thousand dollars. This man spent just shy of seven thousand dollars on me like it was no big deal. Because he "wanted to". What the hell kind of answer is that?

I was already planning on inviting him in when we get back to Wintermore to thank him for such a mind-blowing orgasm in the car, but now I have to pull out the big guns first.

"Take that road on the right and just follow it until you get to the parking lot," I say, pointing out the exit to Henry.

He does as I say, peering curiously up the long single-track road. But there's nothing to see but fluffy snow and branches struggling under its weight. Until we turn and come face to face with thousands of Christmas lights, that is.

Henry's eyes light up brighter than all of them combined as he pulls into the parking lot, perfectly parking in the first free space he comes across.

"Holy shit. This is incredible." He gets out of the car and spins around, taking them all in.

Even I can admit that it's pretty; lights of every color hang from the trees, and there's not an inch of the restaurant's façade not glowing or twinkling.

"What is this place?" Henry asks, his face illuminated by the blue lights on the branch above him.

"Just wait until you see the inside," I say, holding out my hand without thinking. I almost snatch it back, because logic tells me that holding his hand is significantly more intimate than coming all over his fingers a couple of hours ago, but Henry takes it, engulfing my palm.

I lead him across the parking lot, pushing backward through the restaurant's front door so I can watch his jaw drop when he first sees it. And drop, it does. The second we walk into the restaurant, Henry looks like... Well, like a kid in a Christmas themed restaurant, I suppose. He drags his gaze slowly over every inch of the place, taking in the details.

There's a tree at every table, and the ceiling beams are covered in pine garlands and more lights. Ornaments dangle from the ceiling, and the walls are covered in decorations, from giant candy canes to portraits of Santa, to wreaths.

He looks at me with a soft, uncertain smile. "You brought me to a Christmas restaurant? You must hate this."

"I knew you'd love it," I reply, ignoring the part where I definitely hate it. He doesn't, and I like *that*.

His smile stretches into something blinding. "This is... Wow," Henry says as he spots the life-size nutcracker by the door.

The hostess waiting at the stand chuckles, clutching a couple of menus to her chest. "First time?"

I nod, struggling to drag my eyes from Henry. He looks so fucking happy; my heart is damn near beating out of my chest. "He loves Christmas."

"Well, in that case, you've come to the right place. Just the two of you?"

When I confirm, she leads us into the restaurant. "If you don't mind me saying, you're kind of giving me Santa vibes," she says, giving Henry a once-over.

"I've heard that before." He winks at me.

"I'm sure." She's smiling at him, and I have the sudden urge to drag Henry right back out of the restaurant.

Smiling at customers is her job, I remind myself. Not that I should need to remind myself of anything, obviously.

"Rora?" Henry squeezes my hand, and I jump.

"Huh?"

"Is a booth okay?" the hostess asks.

"Sure."

I have to let go of Henry's hand to slide into the booth. The benches are covered in red velvet, but it's not nearly as soft as Henry's suit. We thank the hostess as she sets menus in front of us, and before she's even walked away, Henry reaches across the table to take my hand again.

"You okay?" he asks, his brow furrowed.

"I'm fine." And for a reason I couldn't come up with if you paid me, I force my lips into a strained smile.

This only serves to concern Henry more. Understandable, since I'm not sure I've ever actually smiled around him. It's not like I keep track of when I smile, but it's not often.

I squeeze his hand and focus on the menu in front of me, hoping we can just pretend that never happened. "The menu's Christmas themed, too," I explain, clearing my throat and proceeding to read the menu aloud to him as if he doesn't have his own.

I'm halfway through the entrees when he places his free hand flat on the menu. "What's going on here, sugar?"

I keep my eyes trained on the table. "I'm reading the menu," I reply like it's the most obvious thing in the world.

"Mm." Henry catches my chin with his finger and gently raises my head until I'm forced to look at him. "Yeah, I got that. I was talking more about the little breakdown you seem to be in the middle of."

"Ah, yes. That." I swallow. "I don't really want to talk about that." But it's becoming impossible not to think about, no matter how many kooky Christmas themed menu items I read.

I'm jealous of the hostess. And for what? Because she smiled at a man I barely know? Because she's smiley and works in a Christmas restaurant, and is so much better suited to a man like Henry than me—someone who hates his favorite thing and never smiles?

It's all stupid. Neither of us is well-suited to Henry because he's about to start a job that involves traveling all over the globe, and he doesn't do long distance. And neither do I. Our night together was just us scratching an itch. And the car was … harder to justify.

I barely know him, but I know I like him. Like, *really* like him. *Fuck.*

I sit back against the soft velvet booth and take a deep breath. If I can't turn these feelings off, and I'm not sure I can, I might as well get to know him a little better. This thing between us isn't going anywhere, but we're here now.

"You said earlier that you've been meaning to get a new hobby. What do you do for fun? Watching me aside."

Henry looks momentarily confused at the sudden subject change, but he takes it in stride. "I like to paint. Nothing crazy, just little doodles and stuff like that. It's a stress relief, mostly, but it's so hard to do when I'm traveling. And I listen to a lot of music."

"What kind of music?" I ask, because if I think about him painting, I'm going to think about him *messy,* and that's not a good idea for anyone.

"Anything but acid rock and jazz," Henry replies, wrinkling his nose. "I go through genre phases, but I'll try most things. I can spend hours just listening to a bunch of albums straight through."

"I can't remember the last time I listened to an album from start to finish. I'm more of a shuffled playlist kind of girl," I admit, and Henry laughs, his eyes twinkling sapphire.

"Albums are a dying art, but I like listening to things how artists intended them to be listened to."

"What are your favorites?"

I could listen to Henry talking about the things he loves for hours. I soak in every word, every detail of his face and excited gesture of his hand as he talks me through the albums he's been listening to lately. He doesn't just listen to the music; he analyzes it, going so far as to doing research to find out the context behind the songs.

I promise to listen to some of his favorites, even suggesting we get Noelle to play some at the store. He shuts that down quickly, well aware I'm just trying to wriggle out of listening to Christmas music.

"What about you?" Henry asks once our table is laden down with food. Apparently, my menu-monologuing made everything sound good, and he wanted to try it all.

I spear a maple-glazed parsnip with my fork. "What about me?"

"What do you do when you're not working? The game thing you play?"

I fight a laugh. As much as he looks like a kid on Christmas in here, he's never sounded older. "It's called a Switch, and yeah, that's mostly what I do. I can play it anywhere, so it's perfect for traveling."

"What do you play?"

Trying to explain the concept of *Animal Crossing* to someone who hasn't played a video game in twenty years goes about as well as expected. I pull out my Switch and show Henry my island while we wait for dessert and, once he sees it, he's immediately intrigued. I'm not surprised; he's exactly the kind of person I'd expect to be into cozy games.

Something about sharing little parts of ourselves leaves me feeling simultaneously lighter and heavier as we leave the restaurant, anchored hand in hand. The drive home is far less eventful than the drive to Jackson, and we make it back to Wintermore without incident, listening to a folk album Henry swore I'd like. He was right.

Dusk bleeds over the sky as he pulls into my parents' driveway and kills the engine.

"Do you want to come in?" I ask, my voice suddenly feeling too loud in the twilight hush.

Henry doesn't respond for a moment, and I worry I've seriously misjudged things.

Shit. The way he was holding my hand at the restaurant, the way he slid into the both next to me so we could look at my Switch together and share dessert... I've clearly been seeing something that wasn't there. I should just—

"I do," he replies, finally.

Oh. *Never mind the spiraling, then.*

"But come here. I want to talk first." He taps his thigh.

I unclip my seatbelt, climb over the center console, and settle on his lap.

"This is becoming a habit."

"I don't mind." He cups my chin, his face inches from mine.

I want to pull out my camera and take a close-up picture of his eyes so I can count all the individual shades of blue, so I can zoom in and trace the flecks of violet. But I'm not so far gone that I can't recognize that would be completely unhinged behavior.

"I want to make sure you're inviting me in because you want me to come in and not because you feel any kind of obligation to me for the camera," Henry says, running his thumb across the apple of my cheek.

My skin pebbles under his touch, the sweet scent of him so fucking intoxicating it takes a second for his words to sink in.

I place my hand atop his on my cheek. "I want you to come in because I want *you*, Henry. One night was never going to be enough, no matter how much I tried to tell myself it was."

His fingers twitch against my face, and he sucks in a shaky breath. "I like you, sugar. I can't pretend I don't, but we're both leaving in a few weeks and it's going to hurt like hell."

"Probably," I agree. "I hate goodbyes, but I'm used to them."

My parents went on their first photography trip without me when I was eight months old, and I can't even count the number of times we've said goodbye to each other over the years. And I said goodbye to Wintermore the second I could, but I come back once or twice a year and go through it all over again when I leave the Whittens. They drop me at the airport and I play it cool until I'm out of their sight, then I cry my way through security. Just like every time I see my parents and we part ways. It hurts, but it hurts because I care about them, and that's not a bad thing.

"I'm okay with it hurting later if it means I don't have to hide how much I care about you now."

Henry looks momentarily stunned before a soft, bittersweet smile falls across his lips. "I'm okay with that, too. Let's go inside."

13
HENRY

December 18

I'm on my knees, tying the laces of Rora's boots, when the back room door flies open and Noelle storms in. Rora and I exchange a relieved look; two minutes earlier, and she would have found us in a much more compromising position. We know better than to do this at work, but in our defense, the store only closed ten minutes ago and Noelle doesn't usually finish up for a while after closing.

She drops onto the fraying couch opposite us with a dramatic sigh and a thunderous expression. If this was a cartoon, steam would be billowing from her ears. "I need a distraction so I don't murder my brother."

"What did he—" I begin, but Rora holds a hand up, pausing me. She gives me a look that tells me this isn't the first time she's handled a pissed-off Noelle when it comes to Felix.

"What can we do to help?" Rora asks.

Noelle leans forward, elbows on her knees, her eyes narrowed. "What's going on between you two?"

"What do you mean?"

"I thought this was a one-time thing, but you're really in sync and you're hanging out a lot."

Rora shrugs, toying with the sleeve of her sweater. "We're just enjoying getting to know each other." What a gross understatement.

Noelle groans. "I can't believe this is your first time home for

Christmas in a decade and you're spending more time with my uncle than me."

Guilt rises in my chest. Shit. "I'm sorry. We can—"

"It's not your fault," Noelle interrupts. "It's my asshole brother's. If he actually did his job and ran this place, I might not have to spend every waking moment here and I could spend some time with my best friend who I only see twice a year."

I blink at her outburst, but Rora calmly stands up and walks out of the room without a backward glance. Noelle and I sit in a bewildered silence until she returns all of sixty seconds later, Felix in tow.

"Christmas is in a week. We don't have time for you two to be at each other's throats 24/7, okay? Felix, you're going to pull your weight around here and stop leaving Noelle to pick up the slack," Rora tells him firmly.

Felix crosses his arms, pouting like a teenager. "Or what?"

Rora raises a single brow. "Or I'll tell your dad you're the one who ran over his lit-up gingerbread house."

Felix pales.

Charlie spent months making a life-size gingerbread house for their front yard, only for someone to back into it less than twenty-four hours after his big reveal. It's been over ten years, and he still talks about it.

"Fine, I'll help. What do you want me to do?" Felix asks Noelle.

"I need you to set up the new LEGO display while we're closed tomorrow so I can ship the online orders. And we're not doing Santa pictures on Tuesday, so I need you to clean up the grotto."

Felix huffs, opening his mouth to presumably protest, but one look from Rora and he snaps it closed.

"We can come in and help too," I offer, and Rora nods in agreement.

"Of course. What time do you want us?"

"Oh no, you two are having your days off. Next week is going to be brutal. Take the time to hide away and enjoy … each other, I suppose." She wrinkles her nose.

"Gross," Felix chimes in, but Noelle glares at him.

"You can help me close tonight." She drags him away, shouting goodbye over her shoulder.

"Let's sneak out the back before we get pulled into another sibling dispute," Rora says, leading me out the back door.

In the week since we said "fuck it" and let ourselves have each other, even if only for now, we've settled into something of a routine. I drive us to work in the morning, because Rora needs at least two cups of coffee and three pieces of sour candy before she's road safe, and she drives us back to her place.

Charlie and Kate have been staying in Jackson for a few days, getting Charlie's legs checked out and seeing a Christmas show, so they haven't noticed that I've been sleeping at Rora's. But they got back this morning.

I'm not naïve enough to think we're going to make it through the season without them finding out—I've been looking forward to kissing the hell out of Rora at midnight on New Year's Eve, and there's no way my brother and sister-in-law won't notice *that*—but I'm not sure how I'm supposed to explain it to them.

We're not doing anything wrong, but that doesn't mean they're going to see it that way. They've watched Rora grow up; they're understandably protective of her. It feels pointless to go through the stress of explaining things when this is painfully temporary, but it's going to be impossible not to.

"What do you want to do on our days off?" Rora asks, pulling me out of my head.

"You mean aside from you?"

"I assumed that was implied."

I chuckle, reaching across the car to massage the nape of her neck. She seriously needs a new camera strap, but I don't know how much it would help, considering she spends every day twisting into strange positions to capture the best angles.

Rora groans, and the sound goes straight to my cock.

"I'd like to see your favorite place in Wintermore, assuming you have one."

She glances at me, surprised. "I do have one. We can go there." She turns into the cul-de-sac and squints distastefully at the sheer number of Christmas lights. Most of them are covering Charlie and Kate's house, but every house in Wintermore gets in on the action.

Rora pulls up outside their house and puts the car in park. Now, it's my turn to be surprised.

"If this is your favorite place, then I hate to break it to you, sugar, but I've been here."

She rolls her eyes, the corner of lips twitching. "This is my second favorite place. Although, it temporarily takes first place whenever Charlie makes chili and margaritas."

"He doesn't scrimp on the tequila." The chili is a pale imitation of the one our gramma made growing up, but he serves the margaritas first so no one notices.

"Pack an overnight bag, and I'll pick you up in an hour. We can grab dinner on the way," Rora says, piquing my interest even more.

"You going to tell me where we're headed?"

"Nope. Pack your snow boots."

"You got it." I lean across the console to press a kiss on her cheek, but Rora turns her head and catches my lips with hers.

I knot my hand in her hair, and she whimpers as I slip my tongue into her mouth. Sour watermelon floods my senses, and I already know I'm going to have to stock up on her favorite candy so I can still taste her when I leave. The thought sobers me, and I pull back, swallowing.

I press a kiss to the tip of her nose. "See you in an hour, sugar."

I close the car door, and she pulls away from the curb, flushed.

The house is quiet, and I make it upstairs without running into Kate or Charlie, giving me time to throw a couple of night's worth of stuff in a bag. If I need snow boots wherever we're going, there's always a risk of getting snowed in.

What a shame it would be to get stuck somewhere with Rora...

I'm not so lucky when I make it back downstairs. Charlie, Kate, and the kids are in some kind of standoff. Well, Kate and the kids are standing. Both of Charlie's legs are in casts, so standing isn't really an option.

Kate turns to me. "Perfect. Henry can choose."

"Choose what?" I ask, pushing my duffel bag behind my back as much as possible.

"What you want for dinner," Charlie says. "Noelle and I want to order Thai food. Felix and Kate want pizza."

Shit. "I'm actually not going to be home for dinner. I'm heading out for the night."

Matching looks of suspicion cross their faces. "Heading out where?"

I rack my brain for a reasonable answer; I need to ask Rora how we're handling this going forward. But I don't get the chance to come up with anything before Felix answers for me.

"He has a date with Rora."

Kate claps a hand to her mouth. Still, I decide she's the safer option to make eye contact with.

"Our Rora?" she asks, her eyes widening when I nod. "Wow. That's ... unexpected."

"Unexpected? It's just plain wrong." Yeah, Charlie's pissed. "What the fuck, Henry? She's twenty-eight. And she's practically our daughter! What's next? You're going to date Noelle?"

Jesus.

"Dad!" Noelle injects, tossing a throw pillow at him. "Don't be ridiculous. Yes, Rora is family to us, but Uncle Henry literally met her for the first time a couple of weeks ago. He didn't watch her grow up."

"That doesn't change the fact that she's twenty-eight. You can't possibly be okay with this."

"I'm fine with it," Noelle tells him with a shrug. "Rora asked me before she approached him. You know Rora; you *know* how rare it is for her to be interested in someone. And usually when she is, she's halfway around the world and we have no idea if she's safe. Uncle Henry's a good guy."

"She has a point, honey," Kate chimes in. "We're not upset, Henry. We're just surprised, is all."

"I'm upset," Charlie grumbles, but the heat is gone from his voice.

I take a deep breath, finally turning to address him. "I can't blame you for being upset. I understand how important she is to you, and I know how this looks. But she's important to me too. I've only known her for two weeks, and she's already so important to me. I want to do right by her, and that means trusting her judgment when she says she's comfortable with my age."

Charlie crosses his arms, his face unreadable.

"So, it's serious?" Kate asks gently.

My heart is a lead weight in my stomach. "We're both leaving soon. We're just trying to make the most of the time we have together."

Even I can hear how thoroughly unhappy I am with that answer, and there's a beat of heavy silence before Kate jumps in, sounding much cheerier. "Where are y'all headed tonight?"

I clear my throat, forcing myself to sound less consumed by the deadline on my time with Rora. "I'm not sure. Rora's taking me to her favorite place in Wintermore but won't tell me where it is."

"Oh, you're going to love it," Noelle says. "But make sure you take snow boots."

"And a warm jacket," Kate agrees. "And some blankets. In

fact, I think I'll throw some stuff together for you to take up. I have a bunch of snacks and stuff…" She trails off, heading into the kitchen before I can reply.

The energy in the room has shifted back and forth so much that I'm on the verge of whiplash.

Felix frowns between Charlie and Noelle. "So, are we getting pizza or Thai food?"

14
RORA

December 18

I pull out my phone to text Henry that I'm here, but a knock on the window scares the shit out of me. I jump, dropping my phone on my lap, and look up into Kate's excited face. *So much for picking Henry up without the Whittens spotting me.* How am I going to explain this?

I roll down the window. "Hey."

"Hi, honey. Can you unlock the trunk? I have a bag."

"Um … sure?" I press the button to unlock the trunk, peering over my shoulder, trying to see what she has.

Kate sets two large grocery totes in the trunk, but I can't tell what's in them.

"It's just some extra blankets and candles in case you lose power. You know how cold it can get on the mountain. Oh, and a bunch of snacks and some meals you can cook on the fire if you get stuck. Trust me, you don't want to deal with a hangry Henry."

Well, I suppose I don't have to explain it after all.

"That's great. Thank you," I say as Kate rounds the car and leans in the window.

"You're welcome, honey. Have the best time; Henry's going to love it. Oh, and don't worry about Charlie. He just needs a little time to process. I know you're not really our baby, but we've always considered you one of our own; you know that. It's hard for him to admit you're all grown up. We just love you so much."

What the fuck have I missed?

"I love you, too," I reply because it seems like the safest reply, considering I have no context for what she's saying.

Kate waves, and I reach into the footwell to retrieve my phone. Before I can text him, though, Henry appears, sliding into the passenger's side and tossing his bags in the back seat. He closes his eyes and breathes a heavy sigh, immediately grasping my thigh tightly like he just needs to touch me.

I take a second to look over his profile, backlit by the five billion Christmas lights on the Whitten house. He's ethereally beautiful, and I want to ease every knot of tension from him. How the hell am I supposed to walk away from him in a few weeks?

I place my hand on top of his, rubbing my thumb over his knuckles. "You okay?"

He doesn't miss a beat. "Better now."

"I hear Charlie took it well."

A humorless smile crosses Henry's face, and he opens his eyes, turning his head to look at me. "He took it about as well as expected. He's protective of you. They all are. I'm glad you have them."

"I am too." I bring Henry's hand to my lips, kissing his palm. "But he doesn't have to worry. This is you we're talking about."

I want to say, *He'll come around. He'll get used to it. Give him time.* But what time? In a few weeks, Henry and I will be on different continents, and the only people still thinking about our little winter fling will be us. I'm sure it won't take Henry long to forget it; he'll meet other people while traveling for his new job—smiley, sparkly people who love Christmas and—

"Sugar?"

I startle, looking up at Henry. "Sorry. I zoned out. Let's go." I put the car in drive before I can spiral again, pulling out onto the snow-dusted street.

"What are you thinking about?"

I consider lying, feigning tiredness or hunger, but if Henry and I only get a short time together, I don't want to spend it pretending. "I'm just thinking about what happens when we both leave town," I admit, and Henry's eyes soften into warm pools of blue. "It's stupid. Time is going to pass no matter how much I want to slow it down, and it's only going to pass faster if I'm thinking about what's coming."

"That's true," Henry agrees as we pass through the town center, lights blurring as snowflakes hit the windows and turn to slush. "But if it helps, I've been thinking about it too."

I glance quickly to the side. Henry is staring straight ahead, worrying his bottom lip with his teeth.

"Do you know when you're leaving?" It's the question I've been avoiding since we got home from Jackson and I asked him to come in.

"Not yet," Henry replies, his voice catching. He clears his throat. "My boss said it would be a few weeks before she knows where they're sending me first. Mid-January, most likely."

If he doesn't find out until mid-January, he probably won't be leaving until the end of the month. It's longer than I expected, undoing a few of the thorny knots in my chest.

"What about you?"

"I guess that's the benefit of freelance—I get to decide. I'll reach out to some of my contacts when we know what's happening with your start date. I'm not leaving before you do."

Henry squeezes my knee. "We have plenty of time before that." That feels like an exaggeration, but pointing it out helps no one.

We stop to pick up the Thai food I called in before packing, and in no time at all, we're flying past the *Thanks for visiting Wintermore!* sign.

Henry looks over at me. "I thought we were going to your favorite place in Wintermore?"

"It technically is; it's just not in town," I explain, turning onto the mountain road. It's the kind of road that starts on a slow incline and then suddenly feels like you're driving straight up.

The car lurches and Henry curses, grabbing the handle. "Fucking hell. Is this safe?"

"If you're used to it."

"That better mean you are," Henry says, a white-knuckle grip on my thigh.

No complaints from me.

"I've been driving here since before I had my learner's permit," I promise him, telling him about my mom teaching me the basics of handling a car, in the grocery store parking lot after closing when I was thirteen. Before long, I was driving her up the mountain so she could keep an eye on the surrounding trees for any flickers of wildlife. I swear she can spot a mouse from a mile away. This is one of the few parts of the mountain untouched by Wintermore's Christmas tourism because the road is so treacherous.

The higher we climb, the deeper the snow is. I wouldn't attempt this drive in any other car, but my mom picked this one specifically to handle the mountains in winter. This is her favorite time to shoot, and I make a mental note to send her some pictures when we arrive. Like me, my parents avoid Wintermore like the plague at this time of year; I can't remember the last time they saw the snow here.

I turn off the main road, the car bouncing over the uneven terrain. Henry squints out of the window, but there's not much to see; it's pitch black aside from the headlights shining ahead.

"I promise it'll be worth the mystery when you see it in the daylight," I tell him, slowing the car to take it around a sharp bend.

It's not the first time I've driven this road in the dark, but it's not my preference. I know it like the back of my hand, but there's no guarantee a tree hasn't fallen over the road since I was here last spring.

Our cabin is only a mile up the path, but it's slow going over the snow. I finally park the car, deliberately angling the headlights toward the cabin so Henry has some idea of where we're staying.

He undoes his seatbelt and leans forward, a smile stretching over his face. "Holy shit. This looks like a postcard."

"Just wait until you see the view in the morning. And you don't even know the best part yet."

15
HENRY
December 18

A king bed. A fucking king-sized bed. I love curling up with Rora anywhere, but we're somewhat limited in her twin bed. The things we could do with this much space…

There's no power, but Rora promises that's normal up here at this time of year, and setting the generator up would involve going back out into the snow. We have plenty of candles, lanterns, and an open fire to keep us warm inside. I've slept in far less comfortable places over the years.

I may not be able to see the view, but inside the cabin is picturesque. It's bigger than I expected: two bedrooms, a little kitchen, a surprisingly modern bathroom, and an open-plan living room that's taken up mostly by a large squishy sectional and the bed that's calling my name.

"I come up here whenever I'm home, and Charlie and Kate use it the rest of the year," Rora explains as we make the bed up with soft flannel sheets.

Our dinner is reheating in a pot over the fire, and we stuck a couple of bottles of hard cider in the snow outside to chill.

Once the bed is made, Rora lies down, patting the space beside her.

I stretch out with a groan, twining our fingers together, holding our hands up and watching the shadows dance on the ceiling. "Thank you for bringing me here. I love it."

She rolls onto her front, propping her head up on her hands so she's facing me, her eyes bright in the way I've come to recognize as Rora's version of smiling. I want to commit her expression to memory, burn it behind my eyelids, so I'll still be able to recall every detail of her in six months when these weeks together feel so far away.

"You haven't even seen my favorite part yet. We'll have to wake up early," she warns.

"I can handle early if I get to wake up with you, sugar."

"Charmer." Rora glances over her shoulder at the pot on the fire. "How long until dinner is hot enough?" Her eyes are full of mischief when she turns back, her pupils dilated and cheeks turning pink before my eyes.

I'm pretty sure dinner is almost ready; the scent of ginger, lime, and coconut is already permeating the cabin. My mouth is watering, but not for the Khao Soi bubbling away.

I stand up, the bed creaking, and cross the room. I use the heatproof glove to lift the pot from the grate above the fire and set it on the stone hearth a foot or so away from the flames. Close enough to stay warm, not so close that it'll burn while we're distracted. Because I plan on getting plenty distracted.

I tug Rora to the end of the bed, and she lifts her gorgeous ass in the air so I can pull off her leggings and underwear and toss them aside. I drop to my knees and spread her thighs, devouring her.

She whimpers, pushing back against my face. Her body falls forward against the mattress, her knees threatening to give way. She looks over her shoulder, desperation etched on her face when I pull back and stand up. I walk around the bed, shedding my clothes and tossing my wallet on the nightstand. Rora's eyes follow me every step of the way, her pupils growing.

I lie down and crook my index finger, beckoning her. "Get over here and ride my face, sugar."

Sophie Snow

Rora inhales, licking her lips as she slowly crawls up the bed. She kneels beside me, hesitating. "I … I've never done this."

Fuck. Knowing I'm the first person she's doing this with… *Why is that so hot?*

"You've got nothing to worry about, baby." I sit up and peel her shirt over her head, taking care to graze every inch of skin with my fingertips as I go.

She's blazing hot, her breaths coming short and fast. Rora unclips her bra and throws it to the side before I have the chance. I lean in and circle her nipple with my tongue, tugging gently with my teeth until she's squirming.

I lie back down. "C'mere."

Rora takes a deep breath before swinging her leg over me and hovering above my face. Beautiful mountains surround Wintermore, but this view outdoes them all.

"Fuck, Rora…" I reach up and grip her hips. "Such a pretty, perfect cunt. I need to taste you, baby."

She squeaks as I pull her down and flick my tongue over her clit, teasing her with quick, sporadic licks until the tension eases from her and she sinks down further. And then I snap. Rolling her hips, I devour her. I swear I could get drunk on the taste of her— salty and sweet and *mine*. I pull her forward so I can press my tongue inside her, and she cries out, her hands slamming against the wall.

She's riding me on her own now, so I release my hold on her, sliding my hands down her ass and spreading her. I draw my pinky through her cheeks, teasing her pussy until it's nice and wet, then circle her ass.

"Oh. Oh fuck. *Yes*," she cries, moving faster over my mouth.

That's my girl. I press just the tip of my pinky inside her, very aware that I have big hands. That's all it takes for Rora to freeze, screaming my name as she shakes and comes on my face. I don't stop, licking every drop of her orgasm, savoring her.

God, let her be the death of me. It would be a fucking honor.

I lift her down my body until she's straddling my hips. Grabbing my wallet, I pull out a condom and Rora takes it, tearing into it with her teeth. My skin is crackling with electricity, and I swear I could come just from her rolling the condom over my cock.

I lift her hips so she's positioned perfectly to sink down onto me, and she holds onto the headboard, sinking down slowly with a happy sigh. She feels fucking incredible, her pussy clenching around me. But the sight of her with her head thrown back, sweat glimmering on her chest, her face slack with pleasure, is almost too much to bear. And when she starts riding me... *Fuck.* I almost can't process the fact that I'm here and she's on top of me, and this is actually happening.

Every rise and crash of her body against mine feels like heaven, her thighs trembling around me. She can only sit so high up, but she rolls her hips with each movement, and I think my soul might soar out of my body.

"Damn, baby. Look at you. You're taking me so well."

She responds by drawing her bottom lip between her teeth and riding me faster, harder. I fist the covers, agonizing pleasure lashing me. Rora tilts forward slightly and gasps as she sits back down on my cock.

"Oh god. Fuck, fuck— *Henry*," she cries, coming around my cock with an expression of sheer bliss.

More. I need to see more.

Her movements slow as her orgasm clashes through her, so I grab her ass, moving her over my cock. She falls forward, and I wrap my arms around her.

Her eyes flicker open, hazy and blissed out.

"Give me one more, sugar," I murmur, and they widen.

"I can't. I... *Fuck*," she gasps as I fuck her harder, her eyes rolling back.

"'Course you can, baby."

She whimpers but nods, clasping my face.

"Atta girl."

Whether I can hold out for a second longer is another story. She feels fucking incredible.

Rora takes my lips in a clumsy kiss, and the second my tongue brushes hers, she falls apart, shattering into pieces and taking me right alongside her. I cry her name and she cries mine, and they meet somewhere in the middle where our lips are still pressed together.

Rora's bangs stick to her face, her cheeks are bright scarlet, and she's never looked more beautiful.

And I've never wanted to stop time more than I do right now. I want to stay here, in this moment, for as long as I can, wrapped around Rora, just like it should be.

16
HENRY
December 19

I t's still dark when we wake up to Rora's alarm blaring beside the bed. She groans, burrowing her face against my chest like that will somehow muffle it.

"Should I snooze?" I ask, reaching for her phone.

Rora, I've learned, is an alarm snoozer: she sets her alarm an hour earlier than she actually needs to be awake and snoozes it every ten minutes. I'd hate it if it didn't mean an hour of cuddling every morning.

Rora sits up, her hair messy. She smooths it down, grumbling, "Not today. We don't want to miss it."

She doesn't elaborate, and I immediately forget what she's talking about when she climbs out of bed. She closes her eyes and stretches, not a scrap of clothing to be seen. The last of the firelight illuminates her body, but it's not nearly enough.

I fumble with the battery-powered lantern on the nightstand until it lights up the room. Rora opens her eyes, catching me watching her.

"Enjoying your new hobby?"

"Havin' the time of my life," I say, yawning and reaching for her. "Can't we stay in bed a little longer?"

Rora steps out of my reach. "Nope. Trust me, it'll be worth it. Come on, we probably have enough time to make coffee."

She resets the fire and sets a pot of water on to boil while I rummage around in the cabinets for coffee cups and a French

Sophie Snow

press. We bundle up in sweaters and thermal socks, and Rora
pours the coffee as I drape a blanket over the bench on the porch
so we don't catch hypothermia while we're doing whatever it is
we're doing. It's a covered porch, so it's mostly snow-free, but it's
cold as all get-out.

It's still dark, but Rora wasn't kidding; the view is gorgeous.
Majestic mountains command the horizon. There are miles and
miles of fluffy snow-covered plains between the cabin and the
mountains in the distance, clusters of shadowy evergreens dotting
the landscape. Everything is still and silent, except for the soft
rustling of the pine needles in the nearby copse of trees. The air is
so fresh it stings my nose, bitterly cold with the comforting scent
of pine and snow.

"Shit, it's freezing," Rora says, exiting the cabin. Her camera
dangles from her neck, and she has two steaming coffee cups in
hand. She passes me one and takes the spot on the bench
beside me.

"What are you doing?"

"Sitting down."

I set my coffee on the deck, then pat my lap. Rora rolls her
eyes, but they twinkle as she settles on my lap.

"If my lap is here, that's where you should be sitting, baby," I
murmur, brushing the spot behind her ear with my nose. She
smells smoky and sweet and fucking perfect.

Rora squeals, jumping as I brush a ticklish spot. "You really
are into the whole Santa thing, huh?"

"Not nearly as into it as you are."

She gasps, pulling back to give me a mock glare. "How dare
you."

I laugh, wrapping my arms around her. My coffee is almost
definitely turning icy cold as the seconds tick by, but I'd rather
hold her than drink it.

"It's pretty magical, right?" she says, nodding toward the
mountains in the distance.

I look up, expecting the same landscape I was staring at just moments ago.

But I now understand why Rora wanted to get up so early. Light crests the peak of the tallest mountain, ribbons of hazy pink and yellow streaking across the sky setting the face of the mountains ablaze. It's the most beautiful sunrise I've ever seen, like someone has splashed watercolors across the horizon.

"It's incredible." It comes out in a whisper, the view stealing my voice.

Rora leans into me and I turn away, watching the colors of the sunrise flickering in her eyes. Fuck. *Now,* it's the most beautiful sunrise I've ever seen.

"It's easy to forget everything up here," she says softly, placing a hand over mine. "It's like you're just a smudge on the landscape and nothing else matters. Time just … stops for a second. Everything stops."

She has the same blazing look on her face I've noticed when she catches the perfect shot, and I wonder if time stands still for her when she's behind the lens, too. Anytime I see it, it feels like peering behind the curtain and seeing a part of Rora that only slips out when she's truly in her element.

"Thank you for sharing this with me," I tell her, brushing a finger over the apple of her cheek.

She looks away from the sunrise, meeting my gaze. Whatever expression she sees on my face makes her eyes widen a fraction. She swallows. "I find myself wanting to share everything with you," she says, so softly that even the rustling pines are louder. "And up here… I don't know, maybe it's stupid, but I feel like I can here. Like we can just be here, in this moment, and we don't have to think about what happens when we go back."

I get it.

My brother. Our jobs. Our expiration date. It all seems so trivial here.

"Do you have a place like this?" Rora asks. "Somewhere you can just be?"

"There have been a lot of places—a lot of moments—but I don't have one particular place."

She twists in my lap so she can look at me properly. "Then tell me about your favorite moment. Other than this one, obviously," she quips.

"Obviously," I joke back, even though it's not remotely a joke. This place, this moment, just shot to the top of my list. There's only one other moment that comes to mind, but telling her…

She must see the uncertainty on my face because she prods me in the chest and frowns. "Tell me."

"It's going to sound like a line," I warn, but she just rolls her eyes, gesturing for me to go on. "I was nineteen, and it was my first time out of the country. My first time out of Texas, actually. It was a three-week research trip one of my college professors organized, and I was one of only two lowerclassmen picked to go."

"Where'd you go?"

"The Scottish Highlands," I tell her, smiling as I remember how fucking excited I'd been just to go on an airplane. "It was the middle of November, the lowest temperatures I'd ever experienced, but I couldn't sleep one night, so I went for a walk around our campsite and I saw the aurora for the first time."

Rora barks a surprised laugh. "Seriously?"

"Mm-hmm. It was the most amazing thing I'd ever seen, and I just felt this moment of complete peace." I close my eyes, remembering the feel of the damp, freezing Scottish air on my face. "Twenty-eight years later, and I still remember it like it was yesterday—November, wearing my favorite hand-me-down GAP sweatshirt."

When I open my eyes, Rora's brow has furrowed. "November twenty-third?"

"Yeah. Why?"

She tugs her bottom lip between her teeth. "It's quite the coincidence, is all. November twenty-third, twenty-eight years ago—the first time you saw the aurora, and the day I was born."

There's no way. "Are you fucking with me?"

"Nope," Rora replies, shaking her head and fighting a laugh at the shock I can feel written all over my face. Better shock than everything else I'm feeling; my mind screams at me that there's been a thread of fate tying us together all this time. A cruel fucking thread, all things considered.

"That's some coincidence," I agree, hoping that she can't see just how much it's tearing me up.

Rora settles back against my chest, and we sit in a comfortable silence, watching the sun's crescendo. The wild expanse before our eyes calms me down. I grab my coffee from the deck and sip—ice cold, but caffeine is caffeine.

We didn't bring our phones outside, so I have no idea how quickly time passes as we cuddle and watch the world go by. It's a perfect moment—one I already know I'm going to cling onto for as long as time allows me.

"Hey, sugar?"

Rora tilts her head back to look at me. "Hmm?"

"My memory isn't what it used to be—"

"You are getting on in years. It happens to the best of us. Well, not me yet, obviously."

Lord have mercy. I cover her mouth with my palm, feeling the corners lift below my hand. "Are you done?"

Rora responds by running her tongue along my palm, her green eyes twinkling mischievously. She squeals as I pull my hand away and wipe it on her cheek. "Okay, okay, I'm done."

"As I was saying, I want to remember this moment."

A little of the sparkle disappears from Rora's eyes as the unspoken "when we leave" settles between us.

I run a finger along the edge of her camera strap. "Will you take a picture of us?"

Rora inhales and sits up. "I'd like that. Something to keep."

Something to keep. Because we can't keep each other.

She unwinds her camera from around her neck and turns it on. Her tongue pokes out the side of her mouth, a look of concentration on her face as she messes with the settings. I assume it's still set up for shooting inside the grotto, and it's a hell of a lot brighter out here.

She holds the camera out and then pauses. "You have longer arms."

Rora flips out the screen before handing it to me. Somehow, it's the first time I've held Rora's camera, and holy shit, it's heavier than I expected. No wonder her neck is always sore. It has to be at least five pounds.

I hold it out until we're both visible on the little screen and hesitate with my finger on the button. "I say this with the utmost respect for your craft, but do I just … push the button?" I know photographers who complain about constantly being asked if that's all photography is by people who think anyone could do it with the right equipment.

Rora laughs, a soft, twinkling sound that settles deep in my bones. She so rarely does it.

I think I fall in love with the sound a little more each time.

And I'm going to do myself a favor and pretend that thought didn't just cross my mind.

"Yeah, it's all set. Just push the button," Rora says.

She looks at me with the twinkly almost-smile her eyes do so beautifully, and I press the button without thinking twice. The shutter sounds, and Rora's head snaps around.

"I wasn't read—" Her protest dies on her tongue as the image preview appears on the screen. It's gone as quickly as it appears. I barely see it, but Rora must be used to taking in images in a split second.

"We can retake it," I say, but she shakes her head.

"Let me see."

I hand the camera back, and Rora brings up the picture, holding the screen out for me to look. Our cheeks are rosy red, and there's snow in my beard and in Rora's hair, but those things fade into the background as I take in the look between us, the energy between us. Rora is looking at me with bright eyes and the slightest curve to her lips, like she's mapping every inch of my face. It's my expression that makes my breath catch in my throat, though. Because I've been photographed with a lot of people in my life, and I've never looked at anyone like that.

"Do you have a place like this? Somewhere you can just be?"

I can see it on my face on the tiny screen; I found it. And it turns out it's not a place after all. It's her.

17
HENRY

December 25

We don't fuck around when it comes to Christmas. Charlie and I grew up in a household that took "the most wonderful time of the year" as gospel, and he and Kate have carried on the tradition now that our parents are gone.

When we were kids, Christmas Eve was for caroling, kitchen prep, and Christmas movies. In Wintermore, Christmas Eve is spent working the last shift of the year at The Enchanted Workshop, which closes every year for a week after Christmas.

There were lines out the door yesterday—last-minute shoppers and precocious kids who couldn't understand how I, Santa, could be in Wintermore and the North Pole, getting ready to deliver presents. It's amazing how one simple word—*magic*—can answer every question and make their little faces light up.

Charlie and Kate spent the day at the store, Charlie propped up behind the register with jingle-bell encrusted antlers on his head. By the time Rora snapped the last picture, we were dead on our feet. It wasn't until I was helping her pack up her things that it hit me that the last shot of the night was the last shot of the season.

I couldn't convince Rora to come over and watch Christmas movies with us last night. It killed me, but she doesn't like Christmas, and I'm not going to force it. But fuck, I want her with us today.

It's still dark out, but I can hear someone downstairs, so I jump out of bed and splash cold water on my face before pulling on my red and green plaid family Christmas PJs.

I head into the hall, almost running headfirst into Noelle.

"Merry Christmas, Uncle Henry," she says, pulling me into a hug, practically bouncing with excitement.

"Merry Christmas," I say, but she's already pulling away, bounding down the stairs.

I follow behind her, finding we're the last two up.

I'm helping Felix set the breakfast table when Noelle says, "What's that?"

We all turn to see what she's pointing at: three bags full of presents by the door, wrapped in plain red paper.

"They were sitting on the porch this morning." Kate yawns, stirring a large pot of hot chocolate on the stove. Though she loves Christmas, she's not as crazed as the rest of us and her one Christmas morning requirement is hot chocolate with coffee liqueur.

"Maybe Santa brought them," Felix jokes.

"Pretty sure it was Rora, considering the lack of Christmas paper." Kate smiles fondly at the presents. "We'll drop hers off tomor—"

She doesn't get the chance to finish before Noelle whirls around, hands on her hips. "This is your fault," she practically growls at me, receiving four bewildered looks in response.

"What did I do?"

"It's what you *didn't* do. If Rora dropped these off before we woke up, that means she's not planning to come over today. You had one job!"

That really clears things up. "And that job was…?"

Noelle rolls her eyes like I've missed something obvious. "Make Rora fall in love with Christmas, so she would spend the day with us."

Fucking hell.

"Did you seriously give your best friend the go-ahead to hook up with our uncle so she'd spend Christmas with us? Gross, Noelle," Felix says with a groan.

"In my defense, I thought it would be a one-time thing! And I thought it was working because of the Santa suit—"

"Please stop talking," I beg. It's bad enough that Noelle knows I was wearing it when I went to Rora's; the rest of the family doesn't need to know. "Rora hates Christmas. It's not fair to force it on her if she doesn't want to take part."

Noelle crosses her arms, scowling. "So, you're okay with her spending the day in a big, empty house? All alone? She probably won't even have a real dinner since she hates grocery shopping and all the restaurants in town are closed. And did I mention she'd be all alone?"

Every word chips away at my resolve a little more, and I'm already heading for the door, shoving my feet in my boots, before she's finished. "*When* she's pissed, I'm blaming you," I say, cursing as I open the front door and the air hits my face like an icy shower.

"Just put on the suit, and she'll forget she's mad!" Noelle calls after me as I start down the driveway, my boots crunching in the snow.

Charlie's never going to be able to look at me or Rora the same if he figures that out.

I hurry across the street, grab Rora's spare key from under the plant pot, and head into her place. It's dark and silent, which means Rora probably dropped the presents off early and went back to bed.

Sure enough, she's fast asleep when I step into her bedroom. I grab the tote bag she uses to carry her camera around from the chair by the door and cross the room, taking her phone and Switch from the nightstand and tucking them into the bag. Her blankets are tangled around her feet, which makes it easy for me to hoist her into my arms.

She blinks, bleary-eyed, as I carry her from the room, starting down the stairs. "Am I being kidnapped?" she asks, her voice groggy. She sounds completely unconcerned by the idea.

I chuckle. "If you were, you're doing a terrible job of fighting back, sugar."

"My kidnapper smells good."

We make it outside, and Rora cuddles into me as if trying to get away from the cold. I pick up speed, not wanting her outside for longer than necessary.

"But where exactly are you taking me?"

"You can probably guess."

"I'm still half asleep," she protests, gripping my plaid pajama shirt as I take the porch stairs two at a time.

I push open the door and walk Rora into the kitchen, setting her down in front of my family. *Have they just been waiting?* I swear not one of them has moved.

"Merry Christmas," I say, presenting Rora like a present.

She blinks at the sudden bright light and change in altitude. "Morning," she says, rubbing her eyes. She looks down at herself and pauses. "You couldn't have given me a chance to put pants on?"

I take her in for the first time. I was so focused on getting her over here that I didn't notice that she's wearing only a pair of fluffy pink socks and a maroon t-shirt—my t-shirt. Shit.

Do not get turned on around your family. Maybe they won't notice she's wearing my clothes and it won't be weird. It's so long on her that the hem skims the top of her knees, at least.

"Is that your t-shirt, Henry?"

Well, fuck that, I guess.

I ignore Charlie's question. "Sorry, sugar. I'll go get you some warmer clothes."

I start for the door, but Kate stops me. "No need! We have your Christmas PJs, honey. Felix, they're in the basket beside the fire. Can you grab them? Oh, we're so happy you're here." She pulls Rora in for a hug, breaking the dam.

Noelle is next, then Felix, returning with her PJs. Rora hugs Charlie in his temporary wheelchair, begrudgingly wishing everyone a merry Christmas.

She stands in front of me last, and I don't expect her to hug me in front of my family, given how weird Charlie is being about us, but she does.

I lean down and murmur against her ear, "Merry Christmas, baby."

"Merry Christmas."

"You mad at me?"

"It's cool. I know it was Noelle's idea. She's hard to say no to."

I comb my fingers through the ends of her knotted hair, wishing I could kiss her good morning. But she's not wearing pants, and I don't want to give Charlie any reason to complain on Christmas.

But when Rora heads upstairs to get changed, Charlie looks more confused than concerned.

18
RORA
December 25

I should've known Noelle wouldn't let me skip Christmas Day while I was in Wintermore. And there are worse ways to be woken up than by a six-five man who smells like chocolate plucking you out of bed.

I expected Henry to be more reserved around his family, but he hasn't stopped touching me since I got here—or rather, since he presented me to them. If he doesn't have an arm around my shoulders, he's holding my hand under a blanket or twirling my hair around his finger.

Only once have I been coerced into spending Christmas Day with the Whittens, when I got a mild concussion after slipping on ice and hitting my head on a fence in tenth grade. My parents were out of town, and Charlie and Kate insisted it wasn't safe for me to be home alone with a concussion. I couldn't argue with them, considering standing up to go to the bathroom made me dizzy.

But they've followed the same Christmas Day routine since long before they moved to Wintermore, and today is no exception: breakfast followed by presents, one at a time, so everyone can see each other's reactions, then Christmas music, movies, and so much food there'll be leftovers for a week.

Breakfast was delicious, and I appreciate the boozy hot chocolate for taking the edge off now that I have to watch Henry open

his Christmas present. Thankfully, we saved exchanging gifts for last, and the rest of the Whittens are only half paying attention.

What exactly is the etiquette for giving gifts to the man you're technically just hooking up for the season but have definitely caught feelings for? Finding something he would like wasn't the problem; I'm pretty sure I could just give him a hand-written card with a copy of the picture he took of us at the cabin and he would love it. But finding something that balanced "I know this is just for now, and I'm totally okay with that!" and "I'm pretty sure walking away from you is going to break my fucking heart, and I'm actually not okay with it at all!" was decidedly trickier.

I hold my breath as Henry carefully unwraps the box in his hand, hoping like hell I've made the right call. His eyes widen when the paper slips away, revealing the red and black Switch box, and I immediately go into over-explaining mode. "I thought it would be good while you're listening to albums, you know? When you can't paint, instead of solitaire. Actually, you *can* play solitaire on it, but I figured you might want to mix it up."

A soft smile stretches over Henry's face, the kind that makes my heart skip and my brain conjure up all kinds of alternative endings that won't completely gut me.

"It's perfect. I love it. Thank you." His fingers twitch like he wants to reach for me but is conscious of his family sitting in the same room as us. "You'll need to teach me how to use it properly."

"I will," I promise. "You've already picked it up pretty quickly. And maybe…" I trail off, and Henry raises a curious brow. I almost chicken out because his reaction to what I say next has the potential to split me in two, and I've never been good at hiding my reactions to things. I take a deep breath. "Maybe we could play together. When we're traveling."

Henry just stares at me for a moment, his eyes slowly widening, and I'm sure I've fucked up, come on too strong.

But then he blinks, something else that I don't recognize crossing his expression. "I would really love that, sugar."

I don't even realize how knotted my nerves are until his words sink into me and loosen them. Henry reaches a hand down the side of the couch and picks up a wrapped present. My name is written on the box in his handwriting, but it's wrapped differently to the gifts he gave his family; they were wrapped in red and green paper with foiled Christmas ornaments, and tied with striped ribbon, candy canes, and jingle bells. The Whittens don't half-ass Christmas wrapping.

And Henry hasn't half-assed the wrapping on my gift either, but it's not Christmassy. The wrapping paper is deep purple with a gold sheen and matching gold ribbon, tied with a single white rose and a little pouch filled with my favorite sour candy.

I swallow down a lump in my throat. *He went to all that extra effort just because I don't like Christmas?* Fuck.

"Merry Christmas, sugar," he says, handing it over.

The box is weighty, the paper silky beneath my fingers. I look from the present to Henry. "You literally just bought me a camera; you didn't need—"

"I wanted to get you the camera, and I wanted to get you a Christmas present," he replies so quickly that I'm sure he was just waiting for me to protest. "You can't expect Santa not to get you a present. Open it."

I gingerly unwrap the paper, revealing a sleek golden box inside. I'm hyper-aware of Henry's fingers drumming silently on his thigh. *Is he nervous?* I suppose I can't judge, considering how I felt all of two minutes ago handing him his present.

The lid lifts easily, and I brush away the crinkled paper on top. I can't tell what it is at first, just that it's brown and looks like leather. Reaching into the box, I pull out the gift, and my breath catches in my chest.

"Oh my god."

I run my finger lightly over it, surprised by the tears that threaten my eyes. It's a new camera bag, just big enough for my essentials. It's something I've desperately needed—the bag I have now is great but bulky, and not ideal for smaller shoots. But the practicality of the bag isn't what has me choking up. It's hand-painted, my happy place front and center: the cabin. Above the painting of the cabin, the aurora borealis has been painted, almost identical to my tattoo, except it flows all the way up the bag strap. On the front flap, my name has been embroidered in shimmering golden thread. It's beautiful.

"Henry, I…" I can't find the words. How am I supposed to thank him for something so perfectly *me*?

"There's something inside," he replies softly.

God, this is already so much.

I unclasp the bag and open it to find a matching camera strap painted with the same aurora borealis design. It's a harness style, my name embroidered on the back in the same gold thread.

"I spoke to Bobbi, and she recommended that style since your neck has been getting sore."

"It's perfect. Did you paint these?"

"Yeah…" Henry sounds nervous, and I look up to find him rubbing the back of his neck. It's only been a week since we went to the cabin, and he somehow found time to do this? "I got the bag and strap from Bobbi and painted and embroidered them. I thought it would be good for you to have your place with you, you know, when you're traveling again. It was my first time doing the embroidery, so it's not the best. I wasn't sure if the gold…" he babbles nervously.

Understandable, I suppose, considering the fact that I'm sitting here silently, feeling so fucking *seen*, wondering how I'm supposed to just say thank you when… *Fuck.*

I run my thumb over my name, embroidered perfectly considering it was Henry's first time, and clear my throat. "I'm going to need everyone to cover their eyes for a second."

Charlie groans, and Felix mutters, "Gross," under his breath, but I couldn't care less. I count to five before setting the bag and strap carefully aside and climbing into Henry's lap.

I clasp his face, pressing my nose to his. "Thank you," I say, softly enough for only him. "This is the nicest, most thoughtful gift anyone has ever given me. I love it, and I…" I lose a shaky breath. "I love that I'm going to have my place with me when I'm traveling, yes, but I love that I'm going to have a little piece of you even more."

Henry's eyes are blazing into mine when he cups my face and pulls my lips to his. It could be described as a chaste kiss, if not for the way we desperately grip each other. A split second isn't long enough, but it's all we have at the moment. In the grand scheme of things, it's all we have, period.

I don't want to let him go, but I do. Henry has other ideas, though, clinging to me when I try to climb out of his lap.

Stay. Don't go. He doesn't have to say it; it's written all over this face.

And I want to. God, I want to, but this is already weird for the rest of the Whittens, and me sitting in Henry's lap is probably pushing it.

Henry sighs and loosens his hold on me. I climb out of his lap and snuggle into his side, resting my head on his shoulder instead. It's close, but not so close that it feels like a step too far. He winds his arm around my shoulder and presses a kiss to the top of my head just as Felix grumbles, "Can we open our eyes now?"

"Yeah," I reply, reaching for my new camera bag and taking it in.

The realization is deafening, clanging through my brain like thunder. No matter how much of a lost cause this is … I want to keep him.

19
RORA

December 25

enry follows me into the kitchen, our arms laden down with hot chocolate mugs and snacks plates with nothing more than crumbs and empty candy wrappers left. I dump the mugs in the sink while Henry empties the plates into the trash and stacks them. There are a million dishes to be done, wrapping paper and packaging to be thrown away, and glitter to be vacuumed, thanks to Noelle's wrapping paper choice, but it can all wait. I'll come back in the morning to help clean up.

I stretch my arms above my head as I lean back against the counter, fighting a yawn.

Henry chuckles, bracketing me with his arms. "Sleepy, sugar?"

"Relaxed," I correct, running my hands underneath his shirt, lightly scratching his back.

He hums and ducks his head to kiss the tip of my nose, but I tilt my chin up and capture his mouth. We've been sneaking away for a second here and there to steal kisses all day, acting like those couples in high school that had to find each other between every class because they couldn't spend too much time apart. A lot of couples were like that senior year. There's not much going on in Wintermore, and Wyoming college options are limited. Most people went out of state for college, and everyone knew the odds of their high school relationships surviving long distance. Noelle and her girlfriend spent every second they could together during senior year, then went to colleges on separate coasts and broke up two months later.

I had no illusions that my relationship with Kenny was anything more than a high school fling, so I never really understood the impending doom of graduation day.

I get it now.

Henry tastes like chocolate and peppermint, warm and comforting, and I breathe him in as we break apart, swiping my tongue over his lower lip.

"I should probably go before it gets too late," I say begrudgingly, making no move to untangle myself from him.

Henry frowns, but before I can ask if he wants to come home with me, Kate's voice rings through the kitchen. "It's already late. You should stay, honey."

Henry and I jump apart. Charlie is behind her in his wheelchair, which Felix decorated with tinsel for Christmas.

Where did they even come from? And how long have they been here? *Shit.*

"Oh, uh…" I have no idea what to say here.

"Stay," Charlie says before I have to think too hard. He gives us a wry smile. "I'll pretend you're sleeping in your own room."

I want the ground to swallow me up, but not as much as I want to spend the night with Henry, so I just nod. "That sounds good." I avoid making eye contact with Charlie.

Kate steals Henry to help her move their cars onto the street, since it's supposed to freeze overnight and the Whitten driveway is notorious for turning into an ice rink, leaving me alone with Charlie. Wonderful.

I busy myself at the sink, rinsing hot chocolate residue from the cups and stacking them in the dishwasher.

"Don't worry about that, kiddo. We can get everything cleaned up in the morning."

"I don't mind," I tell Charlie, moving onto the bowls.

"Rora."

"Hmm?"

"I'm sorry."

I pause, the last bowl in my hand.

Damn it. We're going to have to talk about this, aren't we?

I finish up with the bowl and close the dishwasher before turning to face Charlie. "You don't have anything to be sorry for. I'm…" I almost apologize but stop myself. I'm not sorry for anything that's happened between Henry and me. "I know this is weird."

"It is," Charlie agrees. "But I made it weirder by reacting so badly." He crosses his arms and sighs. "It's hard for us—hard for me, I guess. I know you're not really our daughter, but you feel like it. And you're all grown up and traveling the world, which is terrifying and stressful even though we're so proud of you, but you still feel like our little Rora. I love Henry and I trust him a hundred percent, but I can't imagine ever finding out you were seeing someone so much older than you and not finding it difficult."

I pull out a seat and turn it so I can sit facing him. "I don't say this enough, but I've always felt so lucky to have you and Kate. I basically have two sets of parents, and I love you, just like I love my mom and dad. Should I have considered this more before … approaching Henry? Probably, yeah, but I honestly never expected it to turn into this." And I have no idea how to handle it now that it has.

"What exactly is *this*? Because you're both leaving soon, and Henry doesn't…" He trails off, but I can finish the sentence.

"He doesn't do long distance, I know. Neither do I. I know what I want, but I can't see a way to make it a reality, so right now, I'm just going to enjoy the time I get to have with him. We'll try to make it less weird for everyone else."

Charlie gives me a sad smile. "You don't have to. I've seen enough today to know that whatever is between you two… It's a good thing. Don't write it off just because you can't see a path through the trees."

I don't get the chance to process that before the front door opens, Henry's warm laugh washing over me like a ray of sunshine. My eyes are drawn to him the second he walks in the room, his smile making my heart race, as always.

"You ready to head up to bed, sugar? I'm beat."

"Yeah. Night, Charlie. Night, Kate. Love you."

"Love you. Night, honey."

Henry follows behind me as I grab my stuff and start up the stairs.

Charlie and Kate's room is on the ground floor, which is just as well, considering he can't make it upstairs right now. The second floor has three bedrooms. Felix and Noelle's bedroom doors are closed, so they must have come up to bed while we were in the kitchen. My bedroom isn't used much these days, but Charlie and Kate have always promised I'd have a place of my own in their home.

I jump into the bathroom and grab the bag of toiletries I keep here just in case, before heading up to the attic guest room, where Henry has been staying.

I toss my bags on the bed, and Henry wraps his arms around me from behind. "Thank you for today, baby. I know you hate Christmas, but having you around was really special."

His chest is soft and warm as I lean my head back against him, covering his hands with mine. "I enjoyed it."

"Even the Christmas movies?"

"Definitely not. But I enjoyed being with you all. It made me realize I need to make more time for family. When I do come home, I usually keep myself so busy that I never get time to just sit and chill with everyone."

"Does this mean you might come home next Christmas?"

I spin in his hold, tilting my head to look up at him. "Will you be here?"

"Charlie wants us to take turns doing Santa shifts next year. I think he's enjoyed having time off."

"You in the Santa suit? I could be convinced to make an appearance," I say, but I'm already convinced.

Usually, I'd find a photography gig as far away from Wintermore as possible, but even if Henry wasn't coming back next year, I'd probably come home anyway, just for how happy it made the rest of the Whittens this year. I can handle tinsel and candy canes and Christmas music for them.

Henry steps back from me with a twinkle in his eyes. "Close your eyes, sugar."

I raise an eyebrow curiously but walk backward until my legs hit the bed, and sit down, closing my eyes. "What are you doing?" I ask, listening to the rustling of Henry moving around.

"Have you considered having a little patience?"

I'd roll my eyes if they were open.

I feel Henry's footsteps as he crosses the room, stopping in front of me. "Since we didn't get to spend Christmas Eve together..." he says, placing a finger under my chin and tilting my head up.

I open my eyes, and my mouth waters. His Santa suit will be the death of me.

The velvet is perfectly soft as I stand up, running my hands over his jacket. "God, Henry..." I stand on my tiptoes so I can draw my finger along the faux fur band of his Santa hat.

"That's Santa to you, sugar," he murmurs, a wicked smile spreading over his face.

Sweet mother of god.

"Well, *Santa*"—his pupils flare as I emphasize it—"you've been working pretty hard lately. Big time of year for you."

Henry watches me curiously as I spin him around, pushing him down so he's sitting on the end of the bed, but his curiosity quickly morphs into surprise, then desperation, as I drop to my knees in front of him.

"Feels like someone ought to thank you for all your hard work," I continue, watching his breath catch as I part his knees and crawl between them.

I take my time, running my hands up his strong thighs, unfastening the black leather belt around his waist, and pulling the waistband of his pants down. No underwear—why bother?

I wrap my hand around the base of his cock, slowly dragging it up the length and running my thumb across the tip. Henry lets out a shuddering breath. I flick my gaze down his body, making a game plan, so to speak. I've wanted to do this since the second I laid eyes on him, but he's so quick to pounce on me that I've never gotten the chance.

In all the times I've thought about taking his cock in my mouth, I haven't considered the size issue. As much as I love running it, my mouth is on the smaller side. And Henry is … not. But if I don't get him between my lips, I might actually die.

I lower my head, looking up at Henry through my lashes. Any nerves swirling around my stomach disappear when I meet his eye; he looks stunned, like he's never seen something so incredible and he has no idea how to process it. I take it slowly, teasing the head of his cock with the tip of my tongue, but he's already coming undone.

"Fuck," he groans, his hips jumping.

Urged on by his reaction, I lick my way down his length and up again, before finally taking him into my mouth. I can only take him so far and my jaw is going to be sore as hell in the morning, but I wrap my hands around the base of him, drawing them up and down as I bob my head, taking as much of him as I can.

"Rora, baby. Fuck." Henry moans. He looks like he might actually chew through his lip; he's trying so hard to stay quiet. Thank god we're in the attic. He presses a pillow against his face.

I've never really understood the hype around oral, giving or receiving. Henry quickly made me understand the receiving hype, but watching him struggle to keep it together, trying not to lose control, fist my hair, and take over? Oh yeah, I get the giving hype now.

I want to drag it out, to keep him on the edge for as long as I can. As if I can keep us stuck in this beautiful, torturous moment forever. But Henry's thighs are trembling, and I'm not *that* sadistic.

Drawing in a deep breath, I relax my throat to take him as deep as I can. Henry's answering groan is loud even with the pillow, and I'm so caught up in his reactions that it's hard to care about the discomfort of him pressing against the back of my throat. Muffled sounds of what sounds like my name and "fuck" over and over fall from his lips, and I can't help but think he's holding back. Like he's trying *not* to come in my mouth like a gentleman. And I can't have that.

I hum around his cock, tightening my hands around him. Henry goes stock-still before a shiver ricochets through his body and he comes with a gasp, spilling down my throat. I swallow him down, my lungs screaming at me to pull back and take a goddamn breath. When Henry stops shaking, I do, licking every drop of cum from him as I go. We wouldn't want to mess up his Santa pants, after all.

When I'm finished, I look up to find Henry breathing heavily, his arm flung across his face.

I kneel on the bed, leaning down to press a kiss to his forearm. "Still with me, Santa?" I tease.

Henry removes his arm, and I only have a second to prepare myself at the blazing look in his eyes before he's on me, spinning around with a surprising amount of agility, considering how spent he was a second ago. He pins me to the mattress, peppering messy kisses over my face before finally pressing his lips to mine. He runs his tongue over the seam of my lips, groaning as he presumably tastes himself.

Sparks shoot up my body, eliciting a curse from my mouth as he grinds against me. "How the fuck are you hard already?"

"Because," he replies, the words muted because he refuses to remove his lips from me, "you are a goddamn miracle, sugar. Fucking hell."

He sits back on his heels, kneeling between my legs and looking down at me like I really am made of magic. I reach for his cock, resting between us, but he stills me, grasping my hand.

"You reckon you can be nice and quiet for me, baby?" His voice is toe-curling low.

I consider lying; I need him all over me. But being in the attic only affords us so much privacy.

"I honestly don't think I can," I answer, and Henry chuckles, his eyes lighting up like that was the answer he wanted.

He slowly removes the belt from his pants, his eyes never leaving me, and wraps it around his palm. When he slides it from his hand, he flattens it so it's an inch thick.

I realize what he intends before he taps the underside of my chin, and my heart races with excitement.

He brings the belt closer to my mouth. "Open up, sugar."

20
HENRY
December 27

"You want one?" Rora holds up an unwrapped sour candy.

I don't understand how she hasn't fried her taste-buds off with the amount of citric acid she's consumed over the years. Sour has never been my flavor of choice, but it's as close as I can get to tasting Rora on my tongue for now, so I nod.

She pops the candy between my lips, and my eyes water. Rora rests her head on my shoulder, peering down at the Switch in my hand. Charlie and Kate went to visit friends, so she's sitting in my lap in the living room, and we're just pretending that it's not weird that Noelle and Felix are right there.

The past thirty-six hours have been bliss; we've barely spent a second apart. We lazed around with my family all day yesterday, Rora teaching me the basics of how to play *Animal Crossing*. The first thing I asked her to teach me was how to grow flowers, and when she fell asleep, I looked up how to send them to her. If she was serious about us playing together when we're traveling, I'm going to send her virtual flowers every damn day. I'll do anything it takes to keep in touch with her.

We slept at her place because, as nice as the queen-size guest bed here is, she wasn't kidding when she said she couldn't stay quiet, even with the belt between her teeth. And now, she's showing me how to catch fish in the game, and I'm not sure I've ever been so content.

"Okay, hold just a second until—"

My phone rings, and we both jump. I only just manage not to drop the console, but the fish is long gone.

"This is how you know he's old—he has the sound on his phone," Felix grumbles from the armchair, where he was napping before my phone woke him up.

"Everyone keeps the sound on," I say, reaching for my still-ringing phone, but the call ends the second my fingers graze it.

Rora wrinkles her nose and shakes her head. "No one under the age of forty."

"Shit. I *am* old."

Rora reaches up to kiss my cheek. "I like it," she says with a wink, climbing off my lap and stretching. "I'm going to make hot chocolate."

I watch her walk into the kitchen, my heart racing, before glancing at the missed call on my phone. Forget racing; my heart plummets into my stomach. There's only one reason my boss would be calling.

Squeezing my phone tight, I follow Rora into the kitchen. She looks over her shoulder, and I nod to the door.

"I'm going to head out to return this call, so Felix can go back to sleep."

"Cool. You want peppermint in the hot chocolate?"

The bright sparkle in her eyes does nothing to dissolve the dread coiling inside me. I just want to grab her, hide away, and pretend I don't even have a phone.

"Sure, baby. That sounds perfect."

I shove my feet into my snow boots, pull a beanie over my head, and shrug on my jacket before stepping out into the wintry afternoon. The porch roof has done a decent job of keeping the snow off the porch, so I sink onto the swing and take a deep breath before hitting my boss's name.

She answers on the third ring. "Henry! Thanks for calling back. I have your first assignment."

I stay on the porch for longer than I should after the call is over, just processing. But every second in Wintermore feels a little more precious now, and I know better than to waste them, so I stand up and force myself to walk back into the house, stomping my boots on the welcome mat.

Rora is humming my favorite song from the album I played her last night, slowly swaying while she stirs the hot chocolate. She looks up when I enter the kitchen, but every bit of light drains from her face as she takes in my expression. She opens her mouth and closes it again like she isn't sure what to say. The room is silent save for the bubbling on the stove.

"Let's take a walk, sugar."

She swallows and turns the burner off. "Okay." Her hands shake a little as she opens a cabinet and withdraws two travel mugs.

I cross the room, placing a hand on her lower back. "I'll get the hot chocolate."

Rora nods, and I hear her sitting on the bench by the door to pull her boots on. By the time the travel mugs are closed, full of chocolate and peppermint, she's all bundled up. I offer her a cup and she takes it, shouting to Felix and Noelle that we're going out, and threading gloved fingers through mine.

Snow crunches under our boots. We don't speak, just cling to each other's hands and head out of the cul-de-sac. On Main Street, we turn away from the town in unison, an unspoken agreement that we don't want to be surrounded by locals and tourists enjoying the end of the festive week.

We follow the frozen river, and I think we're heading for the park a half mile or so from the town center until Rora tugs me across a small bridge I've never noticed before. She leads me through a tunnel of tall pines and winter shrubs, our tracks the only blemishes on the otherwise perfect snow-covered path. It spits us out into a clearing with an iced-over reservoir and a view of the mountains. A solitary bench peeks through the snow, and small animal print impressions are dotted along the reservoir's edge.

"Jackrabbits," Rora says, the sound startling me. She sets her cup on the snowy bench. "They eat the bark from those plants over there," she continues, nodding toward the trees we've just left. "Their fur turns completely white at this time of year so they're really hard to spot, and I don't know why I'm talking about it so much. Who was on the phone, Henry?" She looks up at me, visibly holding her breath. She already knows where this is going; I just need to rip the band-aid off.

"My boss. She was calling with the details of my first assignment."

Rora looks over my shoulder, then down at her boots. Anywhere but at me. "Where are you going?"

That's not what I expected her to ask. An easier question, with an easier answer than what she really needs to know, I suppose.

I clear my throat. "India. There's a university where one of my colleagues teaches a unit on Arctic research for a couple of months every year, but his wife is pregnant. I have some teaching experience, and they want me to pick up the class so he can stay closer to home."

"Makes sense. You'll be good at that." She blows out a long breath, foggy in the chilly air, before finally meeting my gaze. "When?" Her voice cracks, and the sound cleaves through me with a sharp sting.

There's no happy answer to when I'm leaving, but I know she knows it's an especially shitty answer based on my reaction.

"Friday."

She just stares at me for a moment like she can't process the word that's just come out of my mouth. Her face falls slowly, shadows creeping over her eyes. "Friday? Th-this Friday?" I nod, and she takes a step back like the confirmation has punched her in the gut. "But that's … that's in three days."

She covers her face with her hands, and I want to reach for her, want to pull her into my arms and keep her there for as long as I can. Forever, if I can. But I know she needs a second to process.

"I know, baby."

When she drops her hands and looks up at me, her eyes are lined with silver. "I thought we'd have more warning. I thought we'd get to ring in the new year together. Fuck, I thought we'd have more *time*."

A tear spills down her cheek, and I can't stop myself any longer. I reach for her, tugging her against my chest and squeezing my eyes closed when I feel a sob wrack her body. Rora buries her face against my jacket, and I wrap my arms tightly around her, trying to memorize the feel of her body against mine.

A moment passes, and she looks up at me, her cheeks tear-streaked. "Friday," she whispers like she can't make sense of it.

"Friday," I repeat, my voice thick.

Rora's lip quivers, and I brush my thumb over it, desperate to touch every inch of her.

"I don't know what to say."

There's nothing she can say, nothing that is going to make it any easier when I get on that plane and fly eight thousand miles across the world. This was what I wanted, something new to break me out of my rut. I took this job because she encouraged me to. But now? I don't fucking want it.

I don't want to do this if it means leaving her. I don't want to do *anything* that means leaving her.

"Rora."

She sucks in a deep breath like she can see the crazy ideas running through my head. And they're just that: crazy.

"I already know what you're going to say, but I can't leave without at least putting it out there," I say.

A look of resignation falls across her face, but she nods anyway.

"Let's stay. I'll take over the store so Noelle can open her bakery. You can open a photography business. We could make it work. We could be together."

"Henry."

There's so much anguish in that one word. I clasp her face, pressing my forehead to hers. "I know. I know."

"Neither of us wants that," Rora says, her voice shaky. "We'd just end up resenting this place, resenting each other, like my parents did, because we gave too much up to be here."

"So come with me." The words slip out before I can stop them, and her eyes widen. "I'll be traveling all over. There'll be so many photography opportunities for you." It's not viable. We both know it's not viable, so why am I still clinging to a shred of an idea that it is?

She presses her lips to my forehead, tears running down her face and onto mine. "Three weeks. We only met three weeks ago. I want this, I do, but we hardly know each other. Not enough to take that kind of leap."

"You're right. I know you're right, but god, I fucking hate it."

Rora steps out of my arms, and that little spark of hope fizzles out into nothing. She runs her hands through her hair, chewing her bottom lip. I look away, the tear tracks, the mussed hair, and the hollow expression too much. If this is it, if this is all we get, I don't want to remember us like this.

"I know you were really clear on your feelings on this weeks ago, so there's zero pressure," Rora begins as I stare at a jackrabbit print so hard it blurs. "But what if… What if we tried long distance?"

I look up, but it takes a second for her words to sink in, and she must take my silence for hesitation because she sounds less certain when she continues.

"We could call and video chat, and try to meet up when we

can. We could actually get to know each other and see where this goes. I know you don't do long distance, but—"

"Yes." I don't even have to think about it. As soon as I understand what she's suggesting, it's a no-brainer.

Her eyes widen. "Yes?"

"Yeah, sugar. Let's get to know each other and find a way to be *us*."

She takes a small, tentative step toward me. "Are you sure? I don't want you to agree to this just because it's the only option we have. I know how hard it was for you last time."

I hold out my arms. "C'mere." Rora closes the distance between us, and I fold her into my arms. "I know I said never again, but I didn't know then how I felt about you. It was supposed to be a one-time thing where we went our separate ways. But you're right; this is our only option. Because I have no intention of leaving here without you in my life, sugar. I want you. I want *us*. We don't have to be long distance forever, but we'll get to know each other and we'll figure things out."

"It's not going to be easy," she says, but she sounds a little steadier.

"True. It's probably going to be really fucking hard, actually."

Rora stands up a little straighter, squaring her shoulders. "But we're going to do it."

There she is. Where hope is slowly filling me, Rora is full of that resolved stubbornness that I've come to love so much. *This* is the Rora who wanted a one-time festive fling and made it happen even though it could've turned into an awkward mess. The Rora who snuck into a political rally she wasn't supposed to. The Rora who talks down anxious kids, puts pushy parents in their place, and resolves sibling disputes without breaking a sweat.

And if this is the Rora determined to make things work between us? We've got this.

21
RORA
December 31

As much as I hate Christmas in Wintermore, there's one thing that *almost* makes coming home at this time of year worth it: snow. Getting bundled up and sitting by the window to watch thick flakes drifting by in the wind? The best feeling. Getting an unexpected overnight snowfall so all flights out of Jackson are delayed by at least twelve hours? Somehow better.

But this is Wyoming; snow doesn't keep us down for long, and New Year's Eve finds Henry and me sitting in the airport parking lot, delaying the inevitable. We're not even talking. We're just enjoying our last few minutes alone as best we can. I try to memorize the shape of him behind the wheel, the comforting wall of his body shielding me from the winter sun, and the weight of his hand clutching my knee for dear life.

"What time is it?" I ask, and he grips me harder as he glances at the clock on the dash.

"11:56."

"Oh."

Henry's flight is at 1 p.m. Jackson Hole Airport is small enough that checking your bags and getting through security doesn't take long, but we're pushing it.

And if we don't want to be rushing through our goodbyes…

"We should probably head in," I say, and Henry nods tightly.

He squeezes my knee one last time before letting go and opening the car door.

I barely feel the freezing chill in the air as I step outside, pulling my jacket tighter around myself, purely out of habit. Henry gets his bags from the trunk and closes it with a soft thud. He shrugs his backpack on and shoulders his duffle, holding his arm out for me to snuggle into his side. I loop my arm around his waist. Our height difference makes the walk into the airport clumsy, but I'm not letting go of him until I have to.

How is it possible for this to hurt so much so soon? We've known each other for less than a month. This isn't me. I don't fall like this. It's illogical and terrifying, like something out of the Christmas movies that make me roll my eyes whenever I'm forced to watch them. But those movies always have happy endings, and that brings me a little comfort.

Everything happens too quickly. It only takes a few minutes for them to check his bags in, and we both pretend not to notice how choked up Henry sounds when the person at the desk asks, "Is it just you traveling today, sir?"

And just like that, we're standing outside security. I've stood in this spot a hundred times, on both sides of goodbye, waving off my mom and dad before their photography trips or promising Noelle, Felix, Charlie, and Kate that I'd come home more often, that I'd call more often. I'm used to goodbyes. But this fucking sucks.

Henry takes one look at the entrance to security and turns his back on it, his jaw tight.

"Do you have everything you need?" I ask, toying with the lapel of his rain jacket.

"Everything I can take with me."

I drop my hands and my head, tears springing to my eyes. "Henry." It sounds like a plea. For what, I'm not sure.

He wraps his arms around me, squeezing me tight. "Shit. I'm sorry, sugar. I just… God, I'm going to miss you."

"Is it too late to change my mind?" I ask, tears streaking down my face. "Let's just stay. We'll figure it out." I'm only half joking, desperation taking over.

Henry peers down at me, catching my tears with his thumb. "I don't want something that burns like hell just to fizzle out, Rora. I want this to last. And you were right—we don't know each other enough to jump in heart-first yet. We just have to survive it hurting for a while. It'll be worth it."

"It will," I agree with a shaky breath. Henry runs his fingers through my hair like he's trying to memorize the feel. "And we have a plan."

"We have a plan."

After his class finishes in India, Henry will most likely travel somewhere new every six to eight weeks. We're going to try not to go longer than eight weeks without seeing each other, even if it means we both have to get on a plane from wherever we are and meet halfway for a day or two.

Everything hinges on how quickly things pick up for me once I start my freelance photography. I'm due to leave for my first job in Turin in a couple of weeks, which means two whole weeks of missing Henry in Wintermore.

I'm torn between wanting this new path to take off quickly, because I love my job and I know I can do this, and wanting everything to go nice and slow, so I can work my schedule around seeing Henry. It's stupid and I would never sabotage my career for anyone, but that doesn't stop the heartbroken little devil on my shoulder from telling me there's no point in focusing on my career when, if everything works out between Henry and me, one of us is going to have to compromise, and it really shouldn't be the world-class scientist who's trying to save our planet.

But I owe it to myself to build my reputation up, to make a name for myself outside of corporate journalism. I can't use Henry as an excuse for not trying because I'm scared to get back out there. Photography is in my blood, and no matter what happens between Henry and me, that's one thing that'll never change.

I look over Henry's shoulder, the time on the screen creeping too close to his departure time. We can do this.

"You'll call me when you land in Atlanta?"

Henry cups my face, his fingers trembling. "Of course. And if you're still awake when I land in London—"

"Wake me up if you have to. I'm not acknowledging the new year until I get to do it with you." Henry will be somewhere over the Atlantic when the clock strikes midnight in Wyoming.

"I'll call," he promises. He looks over his shoulder, and when he looks back, his eyes are glassy. "I know you hate goodbyes, so we're not doing that, okay? This is 'see you later'. And you're going to be sick of me by the time we next see each other because I'm going to call you every day and send you pictures of every-thing, even though you'll probably judge how shitty they are and—"

"I could never be sick of you." I wrap him in a tight hug, leaning my head on his chest, feeling his heart race through so many layers of winter clothing. "I'm going to miss you so much. But I'll see you later."

Henry ducks his head to press one last perfect kiss to my lips. "I'm going to miss you, too. So fucking much. I'll see you later, sugar."

He squeezes me then lets go, and I feel like I've been doused in ice when he steps back. One last sad smile crosses his face before he heads into security, and I turn away because I don't think I can handle him looking back. I swear I feel every step he takes further from me tugging on my heart like elastic, ready to snap.

My lip quivers as I walk through the airport in a daze, heading for a quiet spot near baggage claim that my dad showed me the first time we dropped my mom off at the airport together. It's tucked away in a corner, right beside a floor-to-ceiling window with a panoramic view of the runway and mountains beyond.

I sit on the floor, hugging my knees to my chest, and watch the runway through my tears until Henry's plane speeds down the tarmac and flies off. Then, I dry my tears on my scarf and force myself to walk back to the car.

The sun is fiery orange and low on the horizon by the time I pull into the driveway. It's too early for the timer to have switched on the Christmas lights, and I can't bear the thought of going into such a dark, empty house when I feel so fucking empty inside.

I climb out of the car and slam the door behind me, hurrying across the street and up the Whittens' driveway.

The front door opens as I'm stamping my boots on the *Welcome Ho Ho Home!* doormat.

Noelle searches my expression, her face falling at what I'm sure is a tear-stained mess. "You okay?"

I try. I swear I try to keep it together. But she opens her arms, inviting me in for a hug, and I crumble. "Nope," I sob, accepting the hug.

She pulls me into the warm kitchen, pushing the door closed behind us, and pats me gingerly on the back. When we break apart, she somehow already has a tissue in her hand waiting for me.

I dab at my face and blow my nose before exhaling. "Noelle?"

"Yeah?"

"I know it's too early to be sure, but I think I'm falling in love with your uncle."

She wraps an arm around my shoulders, chuckling as she guides me into the living room. "Pretty sure you're the last one to figure that out."

Thu, Feb 9 12:13pm

Are you busy on Tuesday night?

My night or your night?

…

Bear with me. I'll figure out the time zone thing eventually.

And we'll probably just end up in different time zones as soon as you do. You're three and a half hours ahead of me. I was planning to get the train to Hamburg on Tuesday morning, but I can go on Monday instead.

Let's say 5:30 your time, 9 my time. Does that work?

It does. Do I get to see your face?

Sure do, sugar. Can you send me the address of the hotel you're staying at in Munich?

Arnulfstrasse 4, Maxvorstadt, 80335 Munich

Why?

If I don't get to take you out to a fancy restaurant for Valentine's Day, I can at least order dinner for you.

Naughty or Nice

> Hmm, I'm pretty rusty at this, but I think you're supposed to ask me to be your Valentine.

I have a plan. Hold your horses.

Mon, Feb 13 4:29pm

> Did you seriously have my hotel room filled with hundreds of flowers and get the staff to spell out "Will you be my Valentine?" in sour candy on the bed?

If you like it, it was me. If not, I have no idea who it was, but I'm going to have words with them about coming onto my girlfriend.

> I love it. And I love how well you know me. Thank you. Of course I'll be your Valentine.

I wish I could be there in person, sugar. I miss you.

> I miss you too.

> Also... girlfriend?

Are you not my girlfriend? Because I've been telling literally everyone I talk to that you are.

> This is the first time it's come up between us. Girlfriend. I like that.

Good, because I don't think I can stop. I'm considering tattooing it on my forehead.

> Don't do that. The Santa hat will hide it at Christmas. Maybe your cheek?

Perfect. Can't let anyone assume I'm not taken.

> God, the things I'd do to take you right now.

Thanks for making me hard while I'm in a meeting, baby.

Video call me after and I'll take care of that for you.

Fuck. I'll be back in my room in around an hour.

I'll be naked and waiting for you.

RORA
MARCH 7

"Hey, sugar."

The second the video on the screen buffers, I know Henry's had a long day. His face lights up at the sight of me, but his eyes are tired.

I lean closer to the webcam as if that will somehow bridge the gap between Mexico and Canada. "Hi. You look exhausted."

"I know, I know, I'm old. But I thought you liked that about me," Henry jokes, his Texas drawl scratchy. I raise an eyebrow until he sighs, the forced smile slipping from his face. "Jet lag is kicking my ass," he admits, hiding a yawn behind his hand. "But I can handle it. I haven't seen your face in a couple of days, and I want to spend time with you."

"I want to spend time with you too, but you need sleep." I wish I could curl around him and hold him until he drifts off. "What if we both get ready for bed and fall asleep together on camera? I'll be here when you wake up in the morning."

"Isn't it too early for you to go to sleep? It's only eight for you," Henry says, clearly fighting another yawn.

"Sure, but it's me. I love sleep." He still looks unconvinced. "I miss falling asleep with you," I add, and his face softens.

It's the truth, just not a truth I usually let myself focus on because if I do, I'm going to crumble. Every day without him somehow feels worse.

We're both mostly ready for bed, but we brush our teeth and dim the lights. Henry strips off—I don't even pretend not to watch—and I change into one of the t-shirts he left behind in Wintermore for me. They don't smell like him anymore, but I may or may not have made a concoction out of a bunch of Bath & Bodyworks Christmas body sprays until I found something that somewhat resembles Henry's scent: pine, chocolate, candy cane, and cinnamon. I spray it on my pillow every night, which is arguably one of the most insane things I've ever done. But Henry bought several bottles of my favorite lotion before he left because he said he'd miss how I smelled, and I've watched him use said lotion to get off every couple of days since, so at least we're on the same level of unhinged.

We both dim the lights, so it's dark enough to sleep but just bright enough to see each other, and snuggle into our respective beds.

"I miss you so much, baby," Henry murmurs, pulling his blankets up.

"I miss you too. We'll figure out a meet-up soon," I say, but I'm pretty sure Henry was asleep the second his head touched the pillow.

His face relaxes, his breathing evening out. The camera is grainy in the darkness of his room, but I can still see the details of his face: the wrinkles around his eyes, the lines curving around his mouth and nose from that beautiful smile I can't get enough of, and the freckle below his right eye. He looks so peaceful in sleep, so steady.

I stay awake for hours just watching him breathe, understanding why Henry loves watching me sleep so much.

23

RORA

June 9

B etween the spitting rain and bitter wind, you wouldn't know it was June. I trudge up the hill, my hands shoved in my pockets, braced against the wind. By the time I make it up the steep incline, all of five minutes later, the sky is blue and warm sunny rays shine down. This isn't my first time experiencing the whiplash of Scottish weather, but it'll never stop being weird. How the hell do the people who live here know how to get dressed in the morning?

I stare up at the Glasgow Royal Concert Hall, hopping from foot to foot. My phone chimes, and I rummage around in my bag for it, squinting at the message from Noelle.

Did you make it???

I hit *Call* instead of texting back, and Noelle answers on the second ring.

"I'm hoping this is a "yes, I made it, and I'm so excited" call."

Her voice calms me as it sounds through my headphones, but the knots in my stomach are relentless.

"I made it," I confirm, wishing she was here. "I just haven't gone inside yet."

"Why not?"

"What if it's not the same?" It comes out so quietly that I'm not sure she hears me until she sighs my name. "No, I mean it.

What if we don't have any chemistry in person anymore? What if he's forgotten how young I am or he just doesn't like me anymore? What if we don't remember how to be together in person? It's been six months, Noelle. This wasn't supposed to happen."

Eight weeks. That was the deal Henry and I made before going long distance. But we haven't seen each other in person once since our teary airport goodbye, and it's my fault. Kind of. It wasn't intentional; things just took off a little faster than expected with my freelance work. My parents always said it only takes one picture to make a name for yourself, but that you never know which picture is going to be that one, so you should photograph everything. And they were right.

The pictures I shot at the Royal Gala in Turin ended up on the front page of several publications, but those weren't *the* picture. I had a day or two to kill before my flight to Germany, so I wandered off the beaten path into the more local areas of the city. It was on the second day I stumbled upon a woman and her two young children, sitting on the ground outside a church that was handing out food packages. She was making shadow animals on the wall with her hands, and there was so much joy on all of their faces that I couldn't help snapping a picture.

I showed her the preview and she loved it, giving me her email address so I could send her the final picture. I had no plans to share it with anyone else, but I mentioned it offhand during lunch with a journalist friend a couple of weeks later, and everything kind of spiraled from there. It ended up on the front page of a major magazine, and suddenly, my name was everywhere.

Even for viral pictures, the pay is dismal, but I made a decent amount and was able to send every penny to the mom in Turin. My list of jobs built so quickly that I actually had to turn multiple clients away because I didn't have the time. But, like any creative job, you have to capitalize on relevancy before the next best thing comes along, and that meant hopping from job to job and not having any time to meet Henry.

The one time we got close, he ended up stuck in Reykjavik because of a volcanic eruption. We talk every day, but I miss being tucked against his chest, his arms wrapped around me.

Now that we're actually in the same place, though… The doubt is overshadowing the excitement.

"Rora," Noelle chides, exasperated. "It's going to be amazing. This is what you've been looking forward to for literally six months. Look, it might take a day or so for you to re-learn how to be together in person, but you have ten whole days. You're basically all he talks about. He's not going to suddenly decide he doesn't want you. And he hasn't forgotten how old you are because my dad gives him shit for it at least once a week."

I blow out a long breath. "Okay. Okay. I'm going in."

"I'll stay on the phone while you get settled," Noelle offers.

I wish I could hug her almost as much as I wish I could hug Henry. At least one of those things is happening today.

Before I lose my nerve, I hurry up the stairs and into the Royal Concert Hall. When I finally found a gap in my schedule and it lined up perfectly with the end of a climate conference Henry's speaking at here, it felt like fate. I get to see him doing his last talk, and then we get ten days off together.

I stop by the sign-in table, and a woman smiles up at me. "Are you here for the talk on improving monitoring techniques and data in the arctic?"

"My god, that sounds boring," Noelle says in my ear as I confirm I am.

"Great. Can I take your last name?"

"Stanley."

She furrows her brow as she scans a list of names. "I don't have any Stanleys. Are you with the group from Glasgow uni?"

"No, I'm a guest of Dr. Whitten."

Her eyes light up, and she sits back in her chair, giving me a once-over. "You must be Aurora. I swear I feel like I already know you. Henry talks about you so much." She rummages through a box of name tags and hands me one. "He put you under his last name."

Noelle chokes on whatever she's eating, and I have to tune her out to pay attention as I'm directed to the right door.

"He put you under his last name?" she squeals in my ear as soon as I walk away from the desk.

I inspect the name tag, and sure enough: *Aurora Whitten.*

"What was that you were saying about him not liking you anymore? Tell me, when you get married, are you going to take his name or—"

"Shut up," I say, but my stomach is fluttering as I shed my jacket and clip the name badge to my sweater.

"You can't say you haven't thought about it."

I have thought about it. Aurora Stanley-Whitten has a nice ring to it. But if I say that, Noelle will start planning our hypothetical wedding cake before I even hang up.

"I have to go. I'm heading into the auditorium."

"Keep me posted, okay? Everything's going to be fine. Love you."

"I will. Thank you for calming me down. I love you."

I hang up and find my seat in the auditorium, peering down at my perfect view of the stage. The seats fill up, and the butterflies swirl around my stomach. Until the lights dim and the speakers are introduced, and I finally get my first in-person look at Henry in half a year.

He looks better than ever, and I ache with the need to reach for him, to jump down from the balcony and run into his arms.

Soon. I can hold him soon.

The butterflies disappear, and my heart races with excitement. What the hell was I so worried about?

Sophie Snow

If someone had told me last year if I'd be walking into a Climatology Conference After Party buzzing with excitement, I would've questioned their sanity. I weave through the groups of scientists, researchers, and students, searching for Henry. He's so tall that it shouldn't be this hard, but there must be something in the water in the climatology world because everyone here towers over me.

I finally spot him and have to resist the urge to break into a run. He's clearly looking for me, standing with two colleagues I recognize from pictures he showed me from the research station in Greenland.

"Do you want to get dinner after this, Henry?" one of them asks.

I'm close enough to hear them … and close enough to see her touching his arm.

Heat prickles in my chest. I'm too old and too confident in myself to be jealous over a hand on an arm, but I haven't seen him in six months. I can't really be held accountable for my feelings right now.

It takes Henry a second to process what she's said; he's so busy looking around for me. "I can't. My girlfriend is around here somewhere, and we…" he trails off, and his other colleague laughs.

"You're not planning on seeing anything except each other and your hotel room for the next ten days, right?"

"Exactly."

The colleague who asked him to dinner rolls her eyes, but Henry doesn't notice because his eyes land on me. He goes perfectly still for a second before practically sprinting across the room and gathering me into his arms, professionalism be damned.

It feels like I've been holding my breath for six months, and every bit of it comes rushing out now that I'm touching him again.

Henry cups my face, staring down at me like he can't quite process that this is happening. "You're actually here," he murmurs, and his voice washes over me like a warm shower.

"I'm actually here." I don't realize how choked up I am until I hear myself speak. I blink, trying to stop myself from crying happy tears in front of Henry's colleagues.

Ten days is not going to be enough. The words blare through my brain like a siren, and I push them away. I don't want to spend a single second of my time with Henry worrying about goodbye.

I melt into him, the hollow feeling I've been carrying around for months finally gone.

Henry brushes his thumb across my cheekbone, down my cheek, and over my lips. "Hi, sugar."

24
HENRY

June 9

R ora's sitting in my lap, where she belongs, and everything is right in the world. I tighten my arms around her, just breathing her in.

When we were looking for somewhere to stay, we had two criteria: it had to be within an hour of the airport so we didn't have to waste our time together traveling, and it had to have room service because we have no plans to leave this room for the next ten days. Rora found a hotel with lodges that ticked all the boxes, and the view over Loch Lomond is a beautiful bonus.

The second we got to the lodge, I dropped our bags on the floor and pulled Rora to the armchair in front of the window. We've talked every day for six months, but I've been dreaming of holding her since the second I walked away at the airport.

She leans her head back against my chest, and I notice the name tag clipped to her shirt for the first time. *Aurora Whitten.* When the conference organizers asked me if they could just put her under my name, I didn't really think twice about it. Until I did. And then I couldn't stop thinking about it. I don't know if Rora would want to change her name if we ever got married, and I'm definitely getting ahead of myself for thinking about it, but I'm thinking about it. We could always combine names. Dr. Henry Stanley-Whitten has a nice ring to it.

I kiss the top of her head. "I missed you, sugar."

Rora lifts my palm to her mouth and kisses it. "I missed you too," she says with a happy sigh. "Henry?"

"Yeah?"

"I love you."

It takes a second for the words to sink in, her soft voice wrapping me up like a blanket. But when my brain processes the words, I think it might shut down from the sheer serotonin boost.

"You … you…" I stumble through what might go down as the worst reply in history, and Rora sits up, turning so she's straddling my lap, facing me.

"I love you," she repeats, her emerald eyes blazing. "And I know I should probably wait until we have things figured out long distance wise to say it, but I don't want to wait however long that takes."

"Rora. Baby." I hold her face, my voice thick. "I love you so much. So fucking much. I'm pretty sure I've been in love with you since the first time I watched you behind your camera."

Not saying it for the past few months has been torture. It almost slipped out more times than I can count. But I can also see that Rora was right; we needed space and time to get to know each other, and I didn't want to come on too strong, too soon. As shitty as the time apart has been, we've spent hours just talking, learning all we can about each other. And every new facet of her I learn just makes me love her more.

She presses our foreheads together, the tip of her nose grazing mine. "What are we going to do? I love you. I want to actually be with you."

"We both have a month off for Christmas in Wintermore, and we can use that time to figure it out. I already talked to Charlie, and we're going to split Santa duties, and their old photographer should be back so we can have more time together."

Rora laughs, pressing a quick kiss to my lips before sitting back. "Of course you're already talking about Christmas. But that's a good plan. We'll figure things out." Her face falls, and I know she's thinking the same as me: Christmas is months away, which means several more months of long distance.

"We won't go so long without seeing each other next time," I promise.

"I'm sorry," she says, biting her lip. "We said eight weeks, and I completely fucked it up."

"You didn't fuck it up, and you have nothing to be sorry for. Have I missed you like crazy? Of course, but I'm so proud of you for how hard you've been working. And it's paying off."

"But if it means we won't see each other—"

I take her hand, running my thumb over the back of it. Her skin pebbles beneath my touch. "I talked to my boss, and she's going to make sure I have at least a week off between assignments for the rest of the year. No matter where you are, I'll be there. Even if it's only for a day or two." The perks of working for a European company: when they say they value work-life balance, they mean it.

Rora's eyes light up. "Are you serious?" When I nod, it's like months of tension fall from her shoulders. It's not a perfect solution, but it's something, for now.

"Enough talk about what happens after this trip," she says, looping her arms around my neck. "We're here now, and I want to enjoy every second with you."

"Did you have anything in mind, sugar?" I ask, but I'm already standing, lifting her.

She wraps her legs around me as I walk her to the plush king-size bed I barely even looked at when we walked in. And I don't look at it now; how could I possibly look at anything but this incredible woman in my arms? I lay her down, her hair fanning over the covers.

"I have a lot in mind." Rora's back arches as I run a finger down the center of her torso. "But right now, I don't want to take it slow. We've been taking it slow for months. I just need you inside me."

I pause my finger's descent right below her belly button. *Fuck.*

Who am I to say no to that?

I pull Rora to her feet and spin her so I can unzip her dress. It pools on the floor in a ripple of silky blue fabric, and I almost fall to my knees at the sight of her in nothing but light beige lingerie. It matches her skin tone so perfectly she's practically naked. We've seen each other naked plenty since going long distance, but there's no webcam in the world that could do her justice.

Any patience she had left disappears as I unclasp her bra. Rora tears it from her body and throws it away before pushing her underwear down and stepping out of it. She's just as hurried as she rips my clothes off, and I don't have time to blink before I'm standing there in nothing.

A desperate whimper falls from Rora's lips as she sits on the bed, roving her eyes over my body. She scoots back toward the headboard and beckons me. I don't hesitate before kneeling on the bed, the mattress dipping below my weight. Rora watches as I crawl up to meet her, her lips parted, her eyes dark.

She spreads her legs, and she's so fucking wet for me, so ready for me. And I'm so ready to sink into her, to lose myself in her. I fist my cock, running the tip over her until it's glistening with the proof of how badly she wants this.

"Henry, *please*," she begs, squeezing the covers until her knuckles are white.

I press the head of my cock inside her, fighting my body as it demands to fuck her hard, fast, and desperate. Rora might not want to take it slow, but it's been six months and I don't want to hurt her. Nor do I want to come in five seconds flat.

I lean over her, covering her body with mine, and untangle her fingers from the covers. I bring them to my lips, pressing soft kisses to her knuckles, then her nose and her jaw. Finally, her mouth. I slip my tongue between her lips as I push inside her, drinking down her moan.

Rora wraps her legs around me, rocking her hips against me as I bottom out inside her. I inhale a fractured breath.

One, two, three, four… I count in my head, trying not to fall to pieces as she clenches around me. Somehow, I forgot how fucking incredible she feels.

I move slowly, Rora's thighs trembling around me as I pull out and press back inside her.

"Harder," she cries, her cheeks blazing red. "I can handle it."

I'm not sure *I* can, but I'd find a way to give her the goddamn stars if that's what she wanted. "I know you can, sugar," I say, bracing a hand on the headboard and fucking her harder.

Rora's back arches, incoherent sounds spilling from her.

"That's my girl."

She half-opens her eyes, the green bright and glittering against the depth of her dilated pupils. "Say that again."

"You like hearing that you're mine, sugar?" I ask.

She nods, and it's almost enough to tip me over the edge. *Deep, measured breaths.*

I lean in and press a kiss on her forehead. "This beautiful brain is all mine." I kiss her lips. "This perfect mouth is mine." I thrust hard into her. "This beautiful, torturous cunt is mine."

She squeezes me, and I groan her name, my hand slipping from the headboard.

I place it on her chest, her heart beating so hard I'm surprised it isn't audible. "This kind, patient, loving heart… All mine."

"Yours," she gasps, placing her hand over mine.

"And every inch of me, inside and out, is all yours. You own me, heart and soul, baby."

She grips my hand, and I watch her orgasm crash over her for all of a second before I'm right there with her, her pussy gripping me into oblivion. I come with a guttural groan, my body shaking as I try to hold myself up so I don't crush her.

Rora twists in the covers, sobbing my name. She clings to me, her grip slowly loosening as she comes down from the high. I roll us to the side so I can hold her tight, and she continues to tremble in my arms.

"That… Fuck." Her voice is barely more than a croak.

"Fuck," I agree, jumping when she grazes my cheek with her fingers. My nerves are lit up, every touch like a beautiful electric shock. I shift so I can pull out of her and still as I do. *Shit.* "Rora?"

"Hmm?"

"I know this is a really bad time to be asking this, but are you on birth control?"

Her eyes snap open. "Shit. We forgot… It's fine. I have an implant. But I've never forgotten before."

"I haven't either." I blow out a relieved breath.

Thank god. The last thing either of us wants to be doing right now is getting dressed and heading out to track down Plan B.

But now that I know we don't have to worry about it… Why is the thought of her dripping with my cum so hot?

I push it down, lying on my back and stretching my arm so she can snuggle into me. "Do you want kids?" It's not the first time I've wondered—she was so good with all the kids she took pictures of at Christmas. But some people just like kids; it doesn't mean they want to raise them.

Rora traces a finger over the ridge of my iceberg tattoo before answering. "I've always wanted to be a mom. I don't know if it's possible to make it work around my job, but I love kids. I just… I love my parents, and I don't resent one second of my upbringing, but I don't think I could do what they did and travel all the time." She peers up at me. "Do you want kids?"

I kiss the tip of her nose before replying. "Yeah. But same as you, I've never known how to make it work around my job. I kind of gave up on the idea a few years ago; I'm not exactly young."

Her eyes twinkle. "That's true. You're pretty old."

I bring my hand down lightly on her ass. "You chose me."

The mischief on her face softens. "Happy I did. Is that an idea you might consider un-giving up on? Once we figure things out job wise, I mean. It's not a deal-breaker for me. I want you, whatever that looks like, and I understand if you're past the idea. But you would be such a good dad."

My heart swells. *Whatever that looks like.* Even long distance, things look pretty good from where I'm sitting. But starting a family with Rora? That looks like something I couldn't even dream up. I've seen hundreds of shooting stars over the years, and I wouldn't even dare wishing for something so out of reach. But she wants that. She wants us.

"I would have a hundred babies with you, sugar."

"I was thinking maybe one or two. You're going to want to go all out for Christmas, and there's only so many stockings we'll be able to hang from Charlie and Kate's fireplace."

I roll over, pinning her to the mattress with my thighs. "Are you telling me that when you think about our kids, the first thing you think about is Christmas?"

She widens her eyes as if realizing that she's voluntarily talking about Christmas without complaining. "Shit. It is. God, I'm not going to be able to hate on Christmas once we have kids, am I? I'll need to make the most of it this year in case it's my last chance."

She's thinking about us having kids that soon? I'm already trying to talk myself down from finding a way to remove her implant right this second. I swear she makes me lose all reason, and I fucking love it.

"So, I guess that means you don't want me to wear the suit for you this year?"

"I didn't say that."

I chuckle and run my finger over the curve of her jaw. "You really think we might have a kid by next Christmas?"

"I don't know. I just know that once we figure things out and we know how we're going to balance everything, I don't want to waste any time."

"Me either," I agree, sitting back so I can spread her thighs further. My cum is leaking out of her, and it's the hottest thing I've ever seen. "You know…" I say, swiping two fingers through the cum and pressing it back inside her.

She whimpers.

"We should probably practice a lot, so we're ready once we have it all figured out, don't you think?"

"Oh god." Rora squeezes her eyes closed, blowing out a long breath before opening them and looking at me through her lashes. She sits up so she can watch me fucking her with my cum-covered fingers. "You want to practice getting me knocked up?" She licks her lips, and I still.

"Fuck," I whisper. "If Santa is your thing, I think I just figured out what mine is."

"A breeding kink, huh? Interesting…" Rora lies back, her eyes blazing as she spreads her legs. She trails a finger down her stomach. "If you want to practice putting a baby in me, you better fill me up even more. I want to be dripping with you."

As if I could ever say no to that.

25

Fri, Jul 18 9:07am

You're never going to guess who I ran into the airport.

Who?

Your parents.

"Hey, sugar."

"Don't 'hey, sugar' me. What do you mean you ran into my parents at the airport?" I can't believe he just casually dropped "I met your parents" over text.

Henry chuckles, the sound warm and soft, and fuck, I already miss him. He only left yesterday, but I want him back.

"I was grabbing coffee on my way out of the airport when your mom tapped me on the shoulder. They just flew in from Tunisia, and she recognized me."

What are the odds that my parents would be flying into London at the exact same time Henry got in on a layover?

"I can't believe you met my parents for the first time without me there. Was it okay? Were they nice to you?"

My dad is pretty laid back, but my mom? Not so much. And I haven't been able to gauge how she feels about me being with someone so much older over the phone.

"They were nice, baby," he assures me. "They seemed excited to meet me. And I'm glad I got to meet them too, even if you're not here. We're going to get dinner tonight before my next flight."

"That has to be a good sign. I wish I could be there."

"I do too. And not just because your mom is a little scary and I'm pretty sure she's going to grill me tonight."

"She definitely is."

Henry groans, but there's no heat in it. "Any advice?"

"Just don't bring up anything to do with Christmas."

Fri, Jul 18 3:42pm

MOM

Henry's great, honey! We really like him.

DAD

You've got a good one there, Ror.

> Were you nice to him???

MOM

Of course we were!

And he lights up when he talks about you. It's clear he's smitten.

DAD

We're going to try to make it to Wintermore for Christmas so we can spend some time with you both together.

> But you hate going home for Christmas.

MOM

True, but we love you more than we hate Christmas.

DAD

And Henry made it sound not so bad.

Fri, Jul 18 3:50pm

I don't know what you did or how you did it, but you're a miracle worker. I love you so much.

RORA
AUGUST 13

I watch Henry pick up his phone; I see his finger poised to strike the screen; I know it's coming. But nothing could prepare my body for the immediate explosion when he drags the speed of the vibrator up.

The orgasm hits me with a bang, rolling through me, deep and rumbly. My eyes fight to close, my body trembling with the urge to collapse against the bed. But I force myself to stay sitting, my eyes trained on my laptop. I don't want to miss a split second of Henry drawing his fist up and down his cock.

Even with thousands of miles between us, I feel the heat of his gaze all over me. He pulls his bottom lip between his teeth, a groan slipping from his tongue as he watches me shake.

"Fuck, baby. Look at you."

"This… this is what you do to me," I stammer, my vision blurring at the edges.

Henry comes with a cry of my name, my words his undoing. And the sight of him, of his cum shooting across his bare chest, is mine.

Another shockwave courses through me, this orgasm building

more slowly before exploding over my body. I can't stop myself from falling back against the pillows this time.

"You look so damn good. It's driving me crazy, not being able to touch you," Henry murmurs, his low drawl almost enough to send my second orgasm into a third. But I'm spent, and the reality that he's not here creeps in faster and faster every time we do this. I breathe through the last of the orgasm as Henry slowly turns down the vibrator, inhaling the sprayed-scent of him on the hotel pillows, and tug my laptop closer. Henry grabs a box of tissues from the nightstand and cleans his chest.

"If I was there, I could do that with my tongue," I say, sleepily, and Henry raises a brow.

"I *just* finished. Give me a chance to recover before you start talking like that."

I chuckle, but even I can hear how forced it is. Henry doesn't have to ask if I'm okay; I know him well enough to read the question on his face. "I just miss you. I hate being so far away."

The longing in Henry's eyes matches the longing in my heart. "I do too. But this is just one moment in a long life. We have forever to look forward to, sugar."

Forever. Has anything ever sounded sweeter?

Tue, Sep 26 10:13am

I know I was going to call you after my morning meeting, but they need me to go pick someone up from the airport. Can I call you after?

Wed, Oct 4 6:09pm

That was the best surprise ever, sugar. Thank you for coming to see me. I can't believe I got to spend my birthday with you. Miss you already.

26

HENRY

December 3

F elix peeks into the grotto just as I'm about to head out. "Hey, I know it's closing time, but we have one more family coming by. Are you okay to wait?"

I brush fake snow from my pants and nod, sitting back down. "Sure, but Vaughn already left." Vaughn isn't nearly as good a photographer as Rora, but I can admit I'm probably biased, and Rora is definitely overqualified to be shooting Santa pictures. He's a nice guy, but playing Santa is a lot less fun without her here. She's spoiled me.

"It's fine. They're happy to take pictures on their phone. They're leaving early in the morning. I have some paperwork to do in the back, but give me a shout if you need me."

After last Christmas, the last thing I expected was for Felix to actually step up and start pulling his weight as store manager. I don't know what triggered the change, but it was enough for Noelle to hand over the reins completely and finally put a deposit on a bakery. She's planning a grand opening the day before Christmas Eve, which means Felix has been handling Christmas at The Enchanted Workshop all on his own. Mostly. In the week I've been here, I've noticed Kate hovering around the store a lot more than she usually does.

It's strange being back in Wintermore without Rora, especially considering how many Christmases I spent here before we met. I didn't plan to get here so much earlier, but it's just how things worked out with my last assignment. Rora should be here in a few days, and it's pretty much all I can think about, like a lovesick teenager.

I lean my head back against the headrest and close my eyes. It's been a little over two months since she surprised me by showing up in Svalbard on my birthday, but every time we say goodbye is harder than the last. I knew, the second I kissed her goodbye before her flight back to Oslo, that enough was enough. Now, I just have to get Rora on board. Which means I need her here, in my arms again.

Just thinking about her, I swear I can almost smell her…

Something brushes my knee, jolting me out of a Rora-reverie. I jump, my eyes flying open. I must still daydreaming because how else can I explain Rora here, climbing onto my lap, several days early?

But then she lays a hand on my cheek, and her touch revives me. Somehow, she's here.

"Snoozing on the job, Santa? That's not very festive of you."

My hands don't know where to settle; I need to touch her everywhere, need to prove she's real. "You're here."

Rora unclasps my Santa beard from behind my head and pulls it off. "I caught an earlier flight," she says, leaning in. Her lips an inch from mine, she whispers, "I missed you too much."

"God, I missed you too, sugar."

And then her lips are on mine, and I forget every agonizing second apart over the past year because she's here, she's kissing me. Everything is going to work out.

My hands find purchase gripping her face, holding her to me as our tongues get reacquainted. Rora shifts in my lap, and I moan. She pulls back, panting, her eyes glittering with desire. I frown as she jumps down from my lap, but I've barely opened my mouth to protest when she stops me by lifting her sweater over her head.

"I love you, and I promise we can have a super sweet

emotional reunion later, but if I don't get you inside me in the next sixty seconds, I'm going to lose it," she says, matter-of-factly as she pushes her leggings down.

"You— I— Here?" How the fuck am I supposed to think straight, let alone form full sentences when, five minutes ago, I thought she was on another continent and now she's getting undressed in front of me?

Rora nods, shimmying out of her underwear.

"But Felix— The family coming in…"

"Felix made that up because he knew I was on the way. It's just us here. So, are you going to get out of those clothes for me or what, Santa?"

I love every version of Rora, but this version—the bold, brazen version of her—might be my favorite. It was this version of Rora who took a chance and left me a note asking me to come over. And seeing her back here in the grotto just feels so right.

She drags her eyes up my body as I stand to full height and unbuckle my jacket. I drop it on the throne and pull off my shirt before shrugging it back on, just how she likes it. I kick off my pants and boxers, and Rora groans as she takes me in. She steps forward, pushing me back down on the throne with a hand on my chest, and climbs up, straddling me.

My skin pebbles as she runs her hands over my chest. Rora plucks my Santa hat from my head and tugs it on. It's too big for her, but fucking hell, the sight of her wearing it almost has me coming before I'm even inside her.

"How does the saying go again? Wear the hat, ride Santa?"

Holy fucking shit.

Rora rises up on her knees and sinks down, taking me with ease like it hasn't been two months since we've done this. Her head drops back, and my eyes trace the line of her body, my heart thumping.

She grips my shoulders, bouncing up and down on my cock, her lips pressed to mine as moans and whimpers fall from them in quick succession. She feels like a dream, and I want to make this last, but two months without her was two months too long.

I duck my head, running my tongue along the curve of her breast. Rora groans, and I draw her nipple into my mouth, swirling my tongue.

"Fuck, Hen— *Santa*," she corrects with a cry when I lightly bite her nipple.

I sneak my hand between us, and Rora falters as I press my thumb against her clit.

"You feel so fucking good, sugar. So fucking good," I repeat, the words barely intelligible. I'm so far gone.

I draw circles on her clit and, with my other hand, I guide her hips, moving her over me. Her cries get louder and louder until they stop; Rora stills, falling silent as bliss takes over her expression. Her whole body quivers as she comes, her pussy spasming around me, setting every one of my nerve endings ablaze.

I grab her face as gently as I can and pull her lips to mine, moaning into her mouth as I shatter like glass. Everything disappears but Rora, like she's an extension of me, and I never want to untangle from her.

She pants, wrapping her arms around my neck.

"Welcome back, baby," I murmur, nuzzling my nose against her jaw.

Rora squeezes me. "Happy to be home."

I pull back and raise an eyebrow. "You're actually happy to be in Wintermore for Christmas? Alert the press."

"Wintermore isn't home, Henry. You are."

And just like that, I melt. "Oh, sugar. I've missed you so much."

"I've missed you." Rora bites her lip, her voice cracking as she says, "I … I don't want to do this next year. I don't want to be apart anymore."

"Me either."

"How the hell are we going to figure it out?"

I clear my throat. It's now or never. "You're probably going to be pissed at me, but I kind of already did."

She narrows her eyes suspiciously. "What does that mean? What did you do?"

"Here's the thing: in my new job, I spend eighty percent of my work day sitting behind a laptop analyzing data that other people give me. Which is great; I love data. But I don't need to be on-site to do that. Almost all the meetings I have can be done via video. So, I talked to my boss, and she's more than happy for me to work remotely."

Rora's eyes widen, her mouth popping open. "Are you serious?"

"Dead serious, sugar. There will be the odd occasion I have to visit a site, but it shouldn't be for more than a few days a couple of times a year. The rest of the time, wherever you're working, I'm there."

My boss actually seemed relieved when I floated the idea by her. Apparently, after seeing Rora and me together at the conference, everyone was convinced I was going to quit altogether. Which, admittedly, I would've done if working remotely wasn't an option.

I've had over three decades to build my career, and I've taken it as far as I want to. Rora's just getting started, and I'm so honored that I get to watch her soar.

"I can't believe this. It's… You're not going to get bored running around for my job?"

"Sugar, I could never get bored with you. Whether I'm working in an airport or a dingy hotel, if I get to fall asleep with you all over me, then I have everything I need."

Rora inhales a shaky breath. "We're actually going to be together. Like, in close proximity. Literally together."

"Yeah, we are."

Her eyes are wide and bright and brimming with happy tears, and my heart damn near stops in my chest at the sight.

"I know it doesn't solve everything, but fuck, Henry, I'm so happy."

"We can take a year, be together, and actually have time to talk and figure out how we want to go about having a family. We don't have to spend all our time trying to find time to meet up and being generally miserable because we miss each other," I say as the first tear spills down her cheek. I clasp her face, catching her tears with my thumb. "This past year has been the best year of my life, baby. As hard as it was to be away from you, I love that we got the chance to really get to know each other and I got the chance to fall harder and harder in love with you. But next year? It's going to be so much better."

"I love you so much," Rora says, sitting on my lap in the very same grotto where I fell in love with her one year ago.

I lean my head back against the throne with a happy sigh.

She's here.

And she's mine.

27
RORA
December 4

I wake up to kisses being peppered across my face, Henry's soft beard tickling my jaw.

"Wh-what's wrong?" I ask, opening my eyes just long enough to confirm it *is,* in fact, my boyfriend and not someone who's snuck into the cabin to murder us. But murderers don't usually smell like candy canes.

"Nothing's wrong, sugar. Just something you need to see. Sit up a sec."

I'm still mostly asleep, but I let Henry pull me into a sitting position and lift my arms when prompted so he can tug a long-sleeve shirt over my head. He pulls the covers back and puts socks and snow boots on my feet.

"Bring the blanket," he says, before lifting me into his arms.

I snuggle into the warmth of his chest, listening to the steady beat of his heart.

The mountain air is freezing when Henry opens the cabin door and carries me out onto the porch. I hear the creak of the wood as he trudges down the steps, the soft crunch of snow beneath his boots.

He pauses a few steps from the cabin. "Rora, baby, look up."

I grumble as I drag my cheek from the warmth of his skin. "Wh —" The word dies in my mouth as I open my eyes and look up into the sky. I'm only semi-aware of the blanket slipping from my grip.

It's like someone dragged a paintbrush across the horizon, leaving behind streaks of violet and green. The aurora borealis. No picture, nothing I've ever conjured up in my imagination, comes close to seeing it in person.

"Oh my god," I whisper, but it still feels too loud. "It's... I have no words."

He tightens his hold on me. "I know, sugar."

For a second, the world stands still, and it's just me and Henry and a million little stars in a moment I've been dreaming of my whole life.

"I'm so glad I get to have this moment with you," I tell him. I don't realize I'm crying until a hot tear spills down my cold cheek.

"Me too, baby. All the times I've seen this... Not one of them meant as much as this."

I look up into his face to find silver lining his eyes, his irises swimming with the reflection of the starry sky.

"It feels full circle, doesn't it?"

Henry nods, swallowing. "Like it was an invisible string tying us together all these years." He presses a gentle kiss on the top of my head. "And now, we get to spend the rest of our lives together." As if his words were a cue, snowflakes flutter down from the sky, landing on his hair like confetti.

He crouches down to pick up the blanket and carries me back up the porch steps. I fluff the blanket and pull it over us both when Henry sits down on the bench. We can still see the aurora glimmering over the mountains, the sight breathtaking.

Something about the wonder of it all makes me feel a little braver to bring up the thing I've been avoiding since I climbed onto Henry's lap in the grotto last night.

"Henry?"

"Yeah, baby?"

I hold my breath, the mountain air doing little to untangle the knots in my chest. "What if we didn't take a year to figure out how to start a family?"

Henry's eyes widen a fraction before his mouth curves into a perfect smile. "I'd have a baby with you tomorrow if I could, sugar. If you're ready, we'll make it work."

"Yeah?" I don't dare take a breath yet.

"Hell yeah. It might be hard figuring out how to balance everything at first, but isn't it always? We can travel until we need to stop, then settle somewhere—here, or wherever you're most comfortable. When you're ready to start working again, we'll figure out how to travel with a baby. I'll be a stay-at-home—or hotel, I guess—dad, and you'll make incredible art during the day and come home to us at night."

Deep inside me, surprise and hope meet somewhere in the middle. "You would give up your job to take care of the baby?"

"Getting to raise a family with my favorite person in the world and watch her do her dream job at the same time isn't giving anything up. Rora, I don't want you to compromise on your dreams for one second, whether that's a family, your career, or both. We'll find a way to make it work, and our kids will grow up watching their mom have it all."

He makes it sound so simple, and I know that's not how easy it would be in reality, but for a moment, I let myself pretend.

Once, our babysitter fell through on Charlie and Kate's anniversary, and they took us with them on their date night. We had dinner, saw a show, and all squeezed into a hotel room in Jackson. After sweeping the floor with us all at Monopoly, Kate fell asleep, snuggled into Charlie's side.

Felix, thirteen years old and nursing his first heartbreak, asked his dad how he knew Kate was *the one.*

"I woke up one day," Charlie said, smiling down at her, "and realized there was nothing that mattered more than her. Nothing I wouldn't do for her. Because, in the blink of an eye, she was my whole world. And I was so sure I'd never feel that way about

anyone again until you and Noelle came along. And then Rora. It makes me feel like the luckiest man in the world to get to have that kind of love four times over.

"Your mom... She's given up a lot for us over the years, you know? She packed up and left her family, like we all left Mamaw and Pops, just because I've always dreamed of owning a toy store."

"I wasn't giving anything up," Kate cut in, sleepily, from his side. "When you love someone like we love each other, dreams are a shared thing, and it doesn't feel like you're losing anything when you leave things behind to watch the person you love live their dreams."

That's where my parents went wrong, why it didn't work. Their dreams worked perfectly when it was just the two of them, but neither of them dreamed of being a parent. For them, loving me meant giving something up. They chose me over each other.

There's no fear, no resentment, in Henry's eyes when he talks about leaving his job to be a full-time dad. This is his dream as much as his job is.

"We'll find a way to make it work," I echo, my voice once again thick with tears.

Henry's face lights up, brighter and more beautiful than any aurora. "So, you want to start trying?"

"About that..." I wipe my face with my hands, well aware I definitely look like a teary mess. "The odds of getting pregnant with the implant are, like, less than one in a thousand, but—"

"Oh my god." Henry jolts back, his hand flying to his mouth. "Are you... Are we..."

The second I nod, joy spreads over his face. I can probably blame the hormones for being so worried about telling him; of course he's thrilled. This is Henry.

It feels like the heaviest weight has been lifted from my shoulders, and I can finally be excited about this, about our next chapter.

"How— When—" He opens and closes his mouth, and doesn't seem to know what to do with his hands, so I take pity on him and pull down the blanket enough to lay them on my tummy. There's no bump yet, but he places his hand flat on my abdomen and stares like it's the most incredible thing he's ever seen.

"When I visited for your birthday. I only found out a few days ago, but I'm eleven weeks. You know how I've been really tired for a few weeks and having heartburn? Turns out it's not jet lag." The second I explained my symptoms to a pharmacist in London, she grabbed a test from behind the counter.

Henry looks up at me with concern, and I have a feeling he's going to be online looking at symptoms and how to help me the second we go back inside. "Do we need to be worried about that? Are you feeling okay otherwise?"

"It's normal," I promise him, placing my hand over his. "And I feel better since I started taking prenatals. But we have an appointment on Tuesday with an OB, and she'll check everything over and do an ultrasound and... Honestly, I've forgotten half of the tests and stuff I need. It's been a lot to take in."

"I'm sorry I wasn't there when you found out, sugar. You must have been so stressed."

"I was, at first," I say with a shrug. "But I knew I was coming home to you in a few days, and even though I was a little worried about telling you, I knew everything would be okay. I thought I'd be scared out of my mind at the idea of raising a whole person, but I'm really just excited because I get to do it with you."

"You're going to be such a good mom," Henry sniffs, his voice thick.

"And you're going to be the best dad."

I clasp his face, and a single tear falls from the corner of his eye.

"I'm so fucking happy, sugar."

"Me too." I rest my head on his shoulder, and we both look

out at the mountains. "I can't wait to bring them here. To our place."

"Our place, huh?"

"It doesn't feel like just mine anymore. Nothing does. Everything that means something to me feels like *ours*: you, me…" I look down at Henry's hand on my stomach. "The baby. Ours."

"Ours," he agrees, smiling softly. "So, are you going to make the most of hating Christmas for the last year?"

"I think that ship sailed the day I met you, went home, and looked up Santa porn," I admit. "Who'd have thought?"

Henry chuckles. "I, for one, am glad you didn't let your hatred of Christmas get in the way of your Santa kink."

Rora from last Christmas wouldn't believe where I am now. She had no idea how amazing things would turn out. "To Santa kinks," I say, wishing we had hot chocolate or something to toast with.

"And a happy ending better than any Christmas movie," Henry chimes in.

I cup his face and tug him closer, brushing his lips with mine. "Not a happy ending; this is just the start. A happy *beginning*, Santa."

Henry's smile is blinding. He looks down, rubbing his hand over my tummy. "I guess *Santa Baby* has a whole new meaning this year."

The Spicy Stuff

If you should, for whatever reason, wish to revisit *just* the spicy moments… you'll find no judgment here! But you will find the spicy scenes here:

- Chapter Six
- Chapter Ten
- Chapter Fifteen
- Chapter Nineteen
- Chapter Twenty-four
- Chapter Twenty-five
- Chapter Twenty-six

Enjoy!

Acknowledgments

As I write these acknowledgments, I'm just a couple of weeks away from the one-year anniversary of the day I published my first book. And what a year it's been. I am so grateful to every reader who has taken a chance on one of my books over the past year—you have motivated me to keep pushing, even when I've struggled, and Naughty or Nice wouldn't exist without you.

Thank you to my husband, Kyle, and my best friend, Claire, who kept me sane (ish) while I was writing this, my author besties Emily and Alaina for always being there for me, and Taylor Swift for being the soundtrack to every story.

Thank you my beta readers, Claire, Emily, Molly, Sara, and Hamina for your feedback and helping me shape Rora and Henry's story. And thank you to my incredible proofreader, Nina Fiegl, for helping me polish Naughty or Nice.

Thank you Ellie from Love Notes PR for helping me share this book with the romance community, and my incredible street team for always hyping me up and sharing my books—Abigail, Aimee, Allie, Ash, Caitlin, Charley, Claire, Danie, Demi, Elena, Hayley, Jenna, Jess, Jessica, Karina, Kate P, Kate R, Kayleigh, Lil, Molly, Rebecca, Robyn , Sam, Sarah , Sophie D, Sophie L. I feel so lucky to have you all in my corner.

And lastly, I want to thank the readers who have embraced me and my book babies. Every review, share, comment, and excited DM means the world to me. I hope you love Rora and Henry as much as I do, and I can't wait to keep sharing stories with you.

Love,
Sophie

Sophie Snow lives in Scotland with her husband and cat, Pumpkin (who she loves dearly, even if he does bite.)

She writes spicy romance books with messy, queer characters and too many Taylor Swift references to count. She has been in love with love stories for as long as she can remember, and writing them as songs and novels since she was twelve.

A forest fairy in a past life, Sophie loves spending time in nature, drinking too much coffee, and trying out more hobbies than she can keep up with.

You can find more from Sophie by visiting her website at www.sophiesnowbooks.com, or scanning this QR code:

Printed in Great Britain
by Amazon

52805394R00108